WRAPPED AROUND MY HEART

KELLY COLLINS

To my family who are like the sweet little candies hanging from the tree. I love you.

CHAPTER ONE

JESS

E ight o'clock in the morning was my favorite time of day. Not because I'd already had one perfect vanilla latte. Not because the muffins at Baby Cakes were still warm, although that was a bonus. It was because at exactly eight o'clock every morning, Mark Cantwell walked into the office and smiled, and my life became perfect.

"Good morning, Jess." He sauntered toward me and looked to the coffee pot, which sputtered out his cup of famously strong brew. He liked espresso on steroids. Double dark. Double strong. Double delicious. He claimed it put hair on his chest. Something I didn't doubt but wanted the opportunity to confirm. Mark Cantwell's chest had become one of my many obsessions since I started working for him nine months ago.

And just like every morning, I stood in his way, and he slid his hand across my back while reaching for his favorite mug. The one that said, *Show Me the Money.*

"Grab a cup and come to my office." His fingers breezed slowly across the small of my back and disappeared, leaving me wishing his coffee took longer to brew.

"I'll be right there." If I were a savvy planner, I would put his cup to brew two minutes later, so he'd have to leave his hand on my back. But I was more interested in making sure Mark got everything he needed because at the end of the day, that was my job. My purpose was to ensure Mark Sexy-As-Hell Cantwell's full satisfaction.

I picked up the box of muffins and my notepad on the way to his office. The morning huddle was a ritual I prayed never ended. It didn't include the other brokers in the firm. It was just him and me and a box of muffins for thirty minutes. It was the second-best part of my day. Only second because during this time, he never touched me.

My heels click-clacked across the white marble floor to his office. His desk sat to the side of a wall of windows that overlooked Los Angeles, but it was not that view that took your breath away. Nope, the man in the navy blue suit paired with the simple white shirt and a crimson tie did that. One look at him and you knew you were not dealing with a mere mortal; you were dealing with a financial god.

"Did you send the memo out to the team?"

I placed the box of muffins on his desk and arranged his favorite pumpkin spice muffin on a napkin in front of him. Not because I had to but because I wanted to. I sat with my ankles crossed and feet tucked under the chair as I leaned forward, hating the expanse of desk between us.

"Yes. I'm assuming you're talking about the Christmas bonuses for this year."

"I'd prefer to call them profit sharing."

I reached into the box and pulled out a cranberry orange muffin and picked at the edge. Above the paper liner was the only place a muffin top was acceptable. The snug waistband of my skirt served as a reminder to go easy on the muffins and schedule some gym time.

"I sent the memo out last night." Employees who'd been with the company for a year or more benefit from profit sharing. I'd fallen three months short.

"Not a fan of Christmas?"

"I don't see the point." He shuffled through the papers on his desk and slid one single sheet across to me. "I need you to pull the latest data on this company."

I looked at the name: Braxton, Brix, and Billow. "I pulled it for you last week."

He raised an eyebrow. "And?"

I smiled. "And I'll be happy to pull the numbers for you again." I sipped my coffee and stared at him while he shuffled through another pile of papers I'd left on his desk the night before.

"Thank you." He lifted his head for the briefest of moments and gave me a slip of a smile. I loved this little power exchange we had going. He'd demand, and I'd push back. Not a lot, just enough to get him to smile.

"Is this a hostile takeover?" It was a valid question since the man gobbled up companies like I did chocolate candies.

Mark laughed. "No, it's something new." He brought a pen to his mouth and chewed on the end, then laid it on the desktop. "It's a partnership."

I was tempted to snatch the pen he'd been chewing on but let that thought go. Instead, I leaned in like I would if I were to tell him a secret.

"Can I be candid with you?"

He leaned in like every word I uttered was important. "I always want you to be honest with me, Jess."

I lifted my head so we were eye to eye. "Forgive me for saying, but you don't come across as the kind of man who plays nicely with others."

He looked up at me with eyes the same color as a smog-free California sky. "Oh, I'm really quite good at playing, Ms. Stone."

He only used my last name when he was making a point he didn't want me to forget, but what was his point? His words seemed naughty in nature. Combined with his sly smile, and I was certain he was teasing me.

"I'd love to see that, Mr. Cantwell." I made a note to get him the report within the hour. "But in all honesty, you don't seem the type of man who likes to share, and a partnership implies sharing."

He sat back and folded his arms across his broad chest. The smooth fabric of his custom suit gripped his muscles. "We're talking about two different things. I can play all day and never have to share." He took the last bite of his muffin and watched me for a second. "I never share. Once something is mine, it's mine forever."

A shiver ran down my spine. He was probably talking about money or possessions, but when he looked at me and said those words, my heart beat wildly. What would it be like to be Mark Cantwell's woman for a minute—a day—forever?

When the meeting wrapped up, I had a to-do list a page long. I rose from the chair and smoothed out the creases on my gray pencil skirt. "What would you like for lunch today?"

He stood like he did every morning before I left, and he walked me to the door. "Chinese takeout for two."

"Two?" I asked with an ache in my heart. Did that mean he had a lunch date? I scrolled through his calendar in my head and came up with nothing. I knew everything about his business life and nothing about his personal life. I liked to pretend he didn't have a life outside of work, but that was silly. The man was a walking billboard for successful and virile.

"Yes, Jess, two, and plan to spend your lunch with me. I'll give this sharing thing a try."

My heart leapt with joy. The only time we shared lunch was when a deadline was looming and his upper-level executives met around the conference table. Those days I usually served and cleaned up and took notes. This was different. We would be alone.

Within the hour, I had the report he requested. I'd ordered enough Chinese food for a half-dozen people, and I had looked at the clock on my computer at least ten times, wishing that time would fly by so I'd get another serving of Mark.

It was absolutely insane the way I crushed on him. At twenty-eight, I should be past that stage in my life.

At least I didn't have an entire notebook of newspaper clippings like I did when Justin Bieber was coming on the scene.

Every dime I had as a teenager was spent on *Teen Beat* magazines.

The distinctive ringtone for my sister sounded from the bottom drawer of my desk and pulled me from visions of young singers and hot bosses. Bethany's ringtone was the song from *Jaws* that played just before the sharp-toothed beast ripped apart its prey.

Duuun dun duuun dun duuun dun doo dedoo doo dedoo dede doo chomp.

"Hello, Bethany. What's up?"

"Good morning to you too." A little huff of disgruntlement shaded her voice. "Do you answer all your calls like that? It's a surprise you're still employed."

Taken aback, I replayed the four words I'd said in my head. "Generally, I start with a greeting and then move on."

"With a *what's up*? Real professional there, Jess." In the background was the sound of a vacuum cleaner, which meant Bethany's housekeeper was hard at work.

"First of all, you called my cell and not the office, but I don't want to argue with you about it." Arguing with Bethany was as painful as a root canal without the benefit of Novocain.

"Why change things now? You argue with me about everything."

I took a deep breath and let it out slowly and silently. "How's Ben?" That usually was a good deflection technique. Ask Bethany about herself or her child and she was happy. As long as the world rotated around her, all went well.

"He's out with Sasha." Our mother had raised two children while working full time, but Bethany had had a nanny since the day she brought Ben home four years ago. She traded in au pairs like other people did cars on a short-term lease. Sasha was the newest edition and came from Russia. "I'm not sure she'll last. She's young and inexperienced. She's more of a toy to play with than a role model."

What that said loud and clear to me was she was far too pretty to keep full-time in the house.

"That's too bad. So …"

"Right, back to the reason I called. I wanted to talk about Christmas."

"I've already got your present, so no last-minute wishes." It was the same every year. I'd get her something, and she'd tell me at the last minute what she really wanted, which I'd run out and get. Then, on Christmas morning, it was always wrong. The right brand, but the wrong color. The right idea, but the wrong brand. When it came to Bethany, I was always wrong, but I never stopped trying.

"You're arriving tomorrow, right?"

I looked at my calendar. It couldn't be tomorrow. I hadn't even packed yet, but she was right: Tomorrow was the twenty-second, and my flight left after work.

"I'll be getting in really late tomorrow night."

"I can't wait. I bought you the most awesome gift this year. You're going to love it."

I rolled my eyes. Last year her awesome gift was a jar of Nad's hair remover and a bottle of wrinkle cream.

"I'm excited to give you my gift too." I always did something thoughtful. Last year I had her baby shoes bronzed. She said she loved them, but then pointed out the bubble in the finish.

After years of criticism, I had finally realized that no matter what I gave her—even if it was the Hope Diamond—she would find some flaw simply because the gift was from me.

"What did you get me this year? Stationery?"

I nearly dropped the phone because that's exactly what I had bought her. Personalized stationery on linen paper with embossed envelopes, to be exact. *Now what?* "Of course not." I'd be running out later for a new gift.

"Well, it would have been nice," she said wistfully, as if the gift had been on her bucket list for years. She cleared her throat in that mean-girl-pay-attention-to-me way. "The real reason I'm calling is to see if you want to go in on a last-minute gift to Mom and Dad. As a parent, I understand how taxing raising a family can be. How difficult it is to put yourself first."

I pulled the phone away from my face so she wouldn't hear me groan. "Go on."

"I've purchased a cruise to Alaska for them."

My stomach clenched. "You already purchased the cruise?"

"I knew you'd say yes since you have this big-time job now as some man's secretary." She said the word *secretary* like it was bitter on her tongue.

"I'm an executive assistant, not a secretary."

"It's all the same." I could see her in my head dismissing me with a simple wave of her hand. "Anyway, your half is roughly thirty-five hundred dollars. They are going to be so excited. You can thank me later."

I wanted to hit her now. "Bethany, that's a lot of money." I didn't have thirty-five hundred dollars sitting around with nothing to do. I lived in Los Angeles, which came with a higher salary for sure, but it also came with higher rent, insurance, and food costs.

"Oh," she said in a voice that surely matched her resting bitch face. "Come on, Jess, it's a rounding error. Surely you can fork over a few bucks to make our parents happy."

She knew exactly where to hit a girl, and it wasn't in the gut. No, Bethany reached out and twisted my heart. I wouldn't let her see that I was almost on my knees. Even if I had to take an advance on my credit card, I'd get her the money.

"No, that's perfect. I'll bring the money with me."

"You will?" There was a moment of silence. "Super. Don't forget my present."

I hung up the phone and sunk low in my chair. What the hell was I going to do?

CHAPTER TWO

JESS

I laid out a veritable smorgasbord on Mark's desk with the small white containers opened to reveal sweet and savory dishes.

I moved down the row to give him the names of the dishes.

Beef with broccoli.

Cashew chicken.

General Tso's chicken.

Peking shrimp.

Sautéed eggplant and tofu.

Crispy fire beef.

"This is my favorite." I plucked a piece of beef from the box with perfect chopstick technique and held it to his lips. "You think it's going to be sweet when you first taste it, but it's surprisingly hot."

He took the bite and coughed, then reached for the diet soda I'd put on the desk to extinguish the fire I knew would blaze in his mouth. "Holy hell, that's like a volcano."

"Surprised?"

His tongue darted out to lick his lips, and my knees buckled.

"You always surprise me."

I pulled my chair forward.

"How so?" I was all ears.

"I don't know. You manage to keep me on track. You always go above and beyond what's required and …" He turned from me and stared out the window. "I like you, and I don't like many people."

I reached my chopsticks into the eggplant with tofu. "Mr. Cantwell," I said with a teasing lilt to my voice, "that almost sounded like a compliment."

"Are you in need of a little ego stroking, Jess?" He reached across the desk and stole my piece of tofu before I could get it into my mouth.

"Everyone needs a little stroking sometimes." I couldn't believe I'd said that, and by the expression of surprise on Mark's face, it was apparent he was shocked I'd said it too.

He swallowed and studied me for a moment. "Do you?"

I choked on my next bite and reached for my soda at the same time he did. Our hands touched, and a rod of lightning jolted me back.

He slid the can to the edge of the desk. "Drink before I'm forced to give you mouth to mouth." He lifted his brows.

Our conversation was put on hold when the phone rang. I sprung to my feet to grab the line, but Mark shook his head and pointed back to my seat.

"Cantwell Financial. This is Mark Cantwell."

I gave him a thumbs up, and he smiled. The next words out of his mouth made me smile.

"What's up?" he said to the person on the end of the line. To have a recording of that would have been awesome. I could play it for Bethany so she'd see that casual greetings weren't out of line.

I could only hear the bits from Mark's end of the conversation.

"Yes."

"Seriously?"

"You're kidding."

"That's fantastic."

"Of course. We'll make it work."

"Aspen?"

He looked at me.

"That will be fine."

"See you then."

He hung up the phone and leaned back in his chair. A smile bloomed across his face. "Braxton, Brix, and Billow want to make the deal."

"That's great. What's the deal?"

"We'll be taking over half of their client base. They want to move into a different market, and so the capital they'll earn from the sale gives them the cash flow they need to change directions."

I played with a piece of broccoli. "So it's not really a partner-ship so much as a partial takeover." He snatched the broccoli I'd picked up and plopped it into his mouth. "Hey, that's twice you've taken what's mine."

His smile could make an iceberg melt. "You're right, I'm not very good at sharing, but I'm awesome at closing the deal. This one is huge. It puts me at least a year ahead of growth projections."

"What do I need to do for you?" Our playful lunch had morphed back into a business meeting.

"What are your plans for this week?"

I knew my expression had to look like he'd grown a third eye. "It's Christmas week. I'm heading to my parents' house tomorrow night after work. You approved my vacation months ago."

"I need you, Jess."

I'd long dreamed of hearing those words, but not in this context. "I have a nonrefundable ticket."

"To where?" He pushed the boxes out of the way and opened a folder in front of him. "Where are your parents?"

I set my chopsticks down and thought about what Christmas without my family would feel like. I could do without Bethany, but I'd miss my parents something fierce.

"They're in Colorado."

"How far from Aspen?" He shrugged off his jacket and began to roll up his sleeves, showing me the sun-kissed muscles of his forearms. *When does he have time for sun?*

"Umm, they're a couple of hours south of Aspen in a little town called Glory." Seeing as neither of us was eating anymore, I closed up the boxes and packed everything in the delivery bag.

"Perfect. How about you fly with me to Aspen, and I hire a driver to get you to your parents' in time for cookie making or whatever you do before the holidays."

"Can't this wait until after the new year?"

"No, it's a tax thing. I get the write-off, and he gets the income to show his investors. It's a win for everyone."

I shook my head. "Not for me if I have to give up vacation days and time with my family."

"What if I made it worth your while?" He did that damn eyebrow lift that made me weak in the knees. "What if I offered a bonus and promised to get you home for the holidays?"

"How much of a bonus?"

"Are you negotiating with the master?"

"I read *The Art of the Deal*." I pulled myself up a few inches because looking confident would get me a better offer. *Show no sign of weakness*, I told myself.

"Oh, please. That's a bunch of drivel."

We both looked at the empty space on his desk like there was some invisible chess game and the next move would put one of us in checkmate.

"Entertain me."

His lips turned up at the corners. "I'll double your profit-sharing bonus." He unfurled his fingers like flames would shoot from the tips any second.

I laughed so hard my stomach hurt. "That's a no-win for me since I didn't qualify for a bonus. Two times zero is still zero. Try again, Mr. Cantwell."

"What do you mean, you didn't get a bonus? You've been with me forever." He picked up his phone, but I reached over and took it from him and hung up.

"I've been with you nine months. I'm not qualified for—" I made finger quotes. "—*profit sharing*."

"Who made up that rule?" He pushed his chair back from the desk and stood. The man towered over me when we were both standing, but he downright dwarfed me when I sat.

"Apparently *you* did in order to encourage retention."

"That's a stupid rule." He paced in front of the window. His hand swiped through his dark hair, leaving it deliciously messy.

"I agree."

"How about a performance bonus? I've been known to give them from time to time for those that go above and beyond the call of duty." He leaned against the window and crossed one leg in front of the other.

"I'm listening." A bonus was the answer to my most pressing problem: how to pay Bethany back for the trip she'd saddled me with. At this point, anything would help even if it were a few hundred dollars.

His eyes focused on mine for a minute, then focused on a paper clip on the floor. "How much is a day worth to you, Jess?"

"I'm not very good at valuing myself."

He chuckled and walked forward to rest a hand on my shoulder. "You're priceless. You told me you would be when I hired you, and you were right." He let go and made his way back to his chair. "But we'll have to put a price on your time and inconvenience. It means spending time with me outside of normal work hours."

"That's a real hardship." My pulse raced at the thought. Maybe I should offer to pay him. That would certainly satisfy my desire to spend more time with Mark, but it wouldn't solve my financial problems.

He gripped the desk. He leaned toward me, with his blue eyes pinning me in place. "This is my offer. Two thousand a day, first-class travel, and the nicest hotel you can book."

"Why would you pay me that much?" Two thousand a day was insane. I was thinking he'd come up with five hundred dollars maximum.

"Because you're worth it."

Warmth flushed my skin.

"We have to stay the night?"

"You know I like to be prepared for my meetings, and I don't want to take any chances on canceled flights, so getting there a day early is important. We can go over what I need on the plane and then have a relaxing evening. You can pick any place for dinner."

"You're taking me to dinner?" A couple days with Mark, dinner, a hotel, first-class flight, and badly needed cash … could it get any better?

"Of course I'll feed you. I don't like my wom—er, my employees to starve."

"Deal." I offered my hand to shake.

He pulled it between his warm palms. "You failed at negotiations, Jess. You're not supposed to take the first deal that comes your way. I would have paid you more."

My hand was completely covered by his. "I would have taken less." Feeling a band of heat travel from his body to mine, I pulled my hand back like it was on fire and regretted the move when the loss of his touch was felt so profoundly throughout my body.

"I guess you'll be busy the rest of the day. I'd like an early morning flight out of Los Angeles. That should get us to Denver by noon, and we can catch the puddle jumper to Aspen." He walked to the door and opened it for me. "You are amazing, Jess. Never let anyone tell you different."

It was like he was in my head and knew exactly what I needed to hear. "Thanks, I appreciate your generosity, especially around the holiday. The bonus will really help."

"I appreciate your flexibility. Email me the details, and I'll meet you at the airport. Tell your family I'm sorry for interrupting their holiday, but this deal is huge."

"I'm sure they'll understand." They wouldn't right away, but he didn't need to know that. Christmas was the only time my family got together. Cheating them of two days would be like asking them to give up a kidney for a pet. They'd grump and complain, but in the end, they would sacrifice the time because they loved me. The same wasn't true for Bethany; she'd use this as a weapon for years to come. But when I handed her the check for thirty-five hundred dollars, it would be well worth tolerating her attitude for me.

I was late getting out of work because there were so many arrangements that had to be made, but that's where I excelled. If he asked me to find water in hell, I'd do it—or I'd die trying.

With our offices a few blocks from Rodeo Drive, I took a detour to Tiffany's. I knew it was stupid to reward my sister's appalling behavior, but sometimes it was less painful to give in—and now that I would be arriving late, I'd need something extra special to smooth her already sandpapered edges.

With little time to spare and the need to replace the stationery for Bethany, I breezed past the guards to the glass case in the back, the one where they hid the almost affordable gifts. I picked out a single charm, one that should remind her of our cherished tradition of cutting down the tree on Christmas Eve. I tucked the small package into my purse and left. It was a gift I wasn't sure she'd appreciate, but she would like the blue box it came in and the fact it was purchased on Rodeo Drive (confirmed by the gift receipt tucked inside).

CHAPTER THREE

JESS

When I walked into Los Angeles International Airport, I found Mark pacing the floor in front of the United Airlines counter.

"There you are," he said. "I'm starving, and I haven't had my coffee yet."

I let out a laugh. "You could have eaten without me, and there's at least a dozen coffee shops on the way to the airport."

His lips fell into a frown. "But I always have my coffee and breakfast with you on weekdays."

"Come on." I threaded my hand through his arm and tugged him toward the first-class check-in. "What would you do without me?"

"I shudder to think what life would be like without you. It would certainly be coffee-less." He disengaged my hold on him and dropped his arm to rest his hand on the small of my back. It was just like at the office, only there was no coffee pot sputtering in the background.

"Oh, please. You survived before I came along." We approached the counter. "Mark Cantwell and Jessica Stone," I told the woman who ignored me and stared only at my boss.

I pulled out my driver's license and waved it in front of her face. She blinked twice and finally looked at me briefly.

Her eyes went back to Mark. "I'll need your ID too, sir."

"Sorry." Rather than move the hand he had on my back, he set his briefcase on the counter and clumsily reached for his wallet with his other hand. "Here you go." He flipped his wallet open to show his driver's license.

"Can you pull it out?"

His rough exhale made the woman's bangs move. He dropped his hand from my body and fished his driver's license out of the soft leather wallet, then laid it on the counter.

"Thank you," she said softly, and then fell silent for a moment as she typed away. "It looks like your flight is delayed due to weather, Mr. Cantwell. Do you have club access?"

"Yes, I do. How long is the delay?" The low timbre of his voice was like a soft caress across my skin; looking at the way the attendant closed her eyes briefly and smiled, I knew she'd been rubbed the right way too.

She sighed like a teenager in love. "Right now, just an hour, but check in with the club concierge and she'll keep you updated."

"Thank you," I told her, but her eyes stayed on Mark.

"Checking any bags?" She looked briefly in my direction, and I wasn't sure whether she was referring to our luggage or me.

Mark looked from his single bag to mine, and then those crystal clear blue eyes lit on me. "Carry-on? It'll be faster on the other end."

"That works."

I snatched our tickets from the love-struck clerk.

With our boarding passes in hand, we made our way to the club.

"I swear the woman was going to faint when you showed up to her counter." I pulled my carry-on stuffed full of presents and clothes behind me.

He looked at me like I needed medical attention. "What are you talking about?"

"The woman checking us in at the counter. I wanted to place a cup under her chin to catch her drool."

"You're crazy. She was just doing her job." He looked over his shoulder and shook his head.

"You can't be blind to how women look at you." I dashed in front of him and handed our tickets and IDs to the TSA agent at the podium.

"I didn't notice."

"Remind me to get you an eye exam scheduled when we return to work after the holidays."

Mark laughed, and the sound warmed my heart. He was such a serious man, so any glimpse of humor was charming. Yesterday he had been a downright comedian with his innu-endos about sharing and playing.

He walked into the club like he owned the place. Of course, Mark would be a member. I was pretty positive he had Grand Poobah status at all the airlines.

We located two side-by-side chairs. "You stay here. I'll get your coffee and breakfast," I told him. After all, it was what I did every day.

He gave me a heart-halting smile. "That's why I need you. You take such good care of me."

I gave him an eye roll and an exaggerated smile. "That's my job."

When I turned away, I saw the women around us looking at him like they were the warm chocolate in a fondue pot, and he was the dipping fruit. I couldn't blame them, really. It had taken me a month to stop tripping over myself each time I walked into his office—another month to stop stuttering when we talked. Over time things had settled into a routine. I still lusted after him, but I did it quietly in my head. I was a realist. Men like Mark Cantwell didn't date their assistants. They kept work and pleasure tightly contained into two different zones. Two different hemispheres, if I were to be honest, because not once had Mark uttered a word about his private life. No mention of family or friends or weekend dates.

When Mark was at work, it was all business except for yesterday. There had been a tiny bit of playfulness in his words—or maybe it had just been me looking for something more, for a glimpse at the man inside the custom suit.

When I returned, there was a stunning redhead in my chair, leaning toward Mark like she was hanging on his every word.

"Your coffee," I said and handed him the double-shot espresso. It was the closest thing to the black sludge he drank in the office every day.

His expression to me was one of gratitude. "Jess, this is Caroline Butler. She runs a brokerage firm in Los Angeles."

I pasted on a smile. The kind of smile I used when someone was annoying me, but I couldn't let it show. "Nice to meet you." She was exactly the type of woman I expected Mark to date: beautiful, sophisticated, dressed in designer labels.

Next, I sat the plate of mini muffins on the arm of his chair. "They didn't have your favorite, but they had blueberry and buttermilk." I picked up my carry-on bag and started to walk away, but Mark reached out and grasped my wrist.

"Caroline was just leaving." He gave her a smile that didn't reach his eyes. It was the same type of smile I'd just given her moments ago. If possible, I fell a little harder for the man I'd never have. "Jess and I have business to talk over."

A flush rose to the woman's face. I was pretty sure she wasn't used to being dismissed. She dug into her bag and pulled out a business card. When she handed it to Mark, she said, "Let's get together for a drink or something." There was an inflection at the end of the word *something* that told me exactly what her version of something was. It included his light blue shirt and slate blue tie lying on the floor next to her bed.

Mark passed her card on to me without a glance.

Caroline Butler rose and walked away, but before she got too far, I said, "I'll try to fit you into his calendar." I could almost feel the daggers slide into my chest.

"You're a bad girl, Jessica Stone."

"Me? Look at you giving her my seat as soon as I leave to get *you* coffee." I slid into the chair next to him and reached over his body to snatch a tiny blueberry muffin.

"Those are mine," he said.

"Not this one. This is mine." I popped the whole thing into my mouth and chewed. Mark didn't take his eyes off my lips.

He picked up the plate and sat it between us. "Jess," he said in a warm, honeyed voice, "I'd share everything with you." He grabbed another blueberry muffin and pressed it to my lips. I swallowed the one I'd pilfered and took a bite of the one he offered. To my surprise, he placed the other half into his mouth. "Delicious."

"Now who's being bad?"

"Me?" he said and then gave me an uncharacteristic wink.

I shook my head. "What happened to my boss? Who kidnapped him and put in a funny doppelgänger?" The minute the words were out of my mouth, I felt bad because Mark did have a sense of humor, but it was almost always buried under his serious, focused-on-business demeanor.

He narrowed his eyes. "Shall we go over the contract?"

I'd totally blown it. Here he was, acting playful and pleasant for the second time in as many days, and I'd killed the mood without thought to my words.

"Of course." I pulled the folder and a pen from the bag. Stiff-backed and heavy-hearted, I went over the contract bullet point by bullet point.

"There's a typo here." He pointed to the place where *fifty percent* was typed. "Make it fifty-one. I never enter a deal where I don't have the control. You should know that."

In the margin, I wrote *fifty-one* and *control*. That much I did know about the man. He seemed to exercise control over everything. What would an out-of-control Mark Cantwell look like? Something told me it wouldn't be pretty, but something else told me it could be fun too.

We went through the rest of the contract, and I tucked it back into the folder. "Another coffee?"

He had already moved on to something else and simply shook his head no. I tucked myself into the seat and watched the planes take off and land.

"Mark Cantwell and Jessica Stone, please come to the concierge desk," a voice piped in over Bing Crosby's *White Christmas*.

He pushed himself into a standing position. "Looks like our flight is ready. I'll meet you up front."

While his long legs took him to the concierge desk, I packed up my things and followed a few minutes later. When I arrived, I found that my first assumption about Mark was correct: Out of control wasn't a good look on him.

"What do you mean our flight is canceled?" His booming voice echoed through the cavernous entryway.

CHAPTER FOUR

JESS

I placed myself between the concierge and my boss. Bailing him out of jail once he got kicked out of the airport would only put us behind schedule. "Did you say our flight was canceled?"

The pug-nosed woman nodded her head. "Yes, I'm sorry. There is a bad storm moving through the flight path from New Mexico and Colorado."

"Perfect," Mark dropped his briefcase to the floor next to his suitcase. "Just perfect. The biggest deal of my career and Mother Nature decides to slap me upside the damn head."

I turned around and placed my hand on his chest. It was an action without thought, but we both looked at where my hand settled directly over his heart. It beat heavily against my palm.

"Why don't you go back to your seat in the club lounge, and I'll figure something out." I moved my hand to his tie and let my fingers feel the silk all the way from the knot to the pointed end. "I promise I'll come up with a plan." It was a lot to promise, but this was obviously important to him.

His tight-lipped expression softened. "Come on, Jess. You're amazing, but you can't change the weather."

He was right. I couldn't change the weather, but I could change how we approached it—literally. "Go grab another coffee. Maybe decaf this time. Give me fifteen minutes."

He nodded his head. "I'll be sulking in the corner."

I picked up his briefcase and handed it to him. "Mark Cantwell doesn't sulk. He conquers, and this isn't an insurmountable problem. It might take a little finessing, but that's what I do. Now go."

I turned him toward the club and gave him a little push. A bolder woman would have swatted him on his ass, but I wasn't that brave. I may have been secretly in love with my boss, but I was also in love with my job. One was a fantasy; the other, a reality.

As soon as he disappeared behind the frosted-glass doors, I went to work. "Can you reroute us around the storm?" I figured if the storm was moving east, I might be able to come at it from the east. If I were lucky enough, I could beat it to the mountains. Once we were there, it didn't matter if it dumped a hundred inches of snow. What mattered was that Mark met this client and signed the deal.

My parents and plans were another matter. Eventually, the storm would clear, and I'd get home, and if luck was on my side, I'd be able to accomplish it all.

Ten minutes later, I rushed into the club to grab my boss. "Let's go. I've got us rerouted through Dallas to Cheyenne.

We'll pick up a car and drive from there. It's less than three hundred miles. We should get there late tonight."

Mark stared at me for a minute. "You got us a flight?"

I folded his newspaper and slipped it into the side pocket of his briefcase. "It's a circuitous route, but it gets us closer than we are now. If we're lucky, we'll beat the storm. If not … I don't want to think about it." I held the handle to my rolling bag and started toward the new gate with him following me. "We need to get to terminal one. We're taking a Southwest flight to Dallas, and a United flight to Cheyenne. We'll rent a car when we get there and drive to Aspen."

"That's a lot of travel."

I was at a half-run, yet it only took his normal stride to keep up with me. "You wanted to get there the night before so you can prepare. I'm getting you there," I said, almost too winded to speak.

We had to cut across the parking garage to get from terminal seven to terminal one. We checked in and raced to the gate, arriving just in time. Shoved into the very back of the plane, we took our seats.

"How the mighty have fallen." Mark took his jacket off and crammed it into what little space there was in the overhead compartment.

"It's not first class, but it will get us closer to the goal." I kicked my carry-on bag under the seat in front of me and buckled up. It was going to be a long two-and-a-half hours. "By the way, why is this particular deal so important?"

Mark settled in and sighed. "My grandfather owned this company years ago. Instead of Braxton, Brix, and Billow, it was Cantwell, Brix, and Atrum."

"Hostile takeover?" It seemed to be how most of these big firms exchanged hands.

"It was hostile all right."

The plane shook and rattled as it raced down the runway. My heart pounded against my chest cavity before it tumbled into the pit of my stomach.

"What happened?" I gripped the armrest so hard my knuckles blanched. Flying was not my favorite thing. I was fine while I was in the air, but the takeoffs and landings always unsettled me.

His eyes went to my white knuckles, and his hand covered mine in a sweet comforting gesture. "The company belonged to my grandfather. It was held in trust for me by my father once Grandfather died, but he was given too much control, and before I could take over, he sold it."

"Your father sold it out from under you?" I was appalled that a parent could be so devious. My parents would have donated their hearts if they thought Bethany or I needed them. They were self-sacrificing, not self-serving. "That's awful."

"I agree." The plane leveled out, and the turbulent start became a smooth flight. Mark removed his hand from mine. "Hostile takeovers—or, in this case, total annihilation—are not uncommon in my family."

I didn't know anything about Mark's family, but this seemed like a good time to get to know the man behind my paycheck and my wildest fantasies.

"Tell me about your family."

He let out a laugh that was a cross between sinister and disbelieving. "I don't have one."

"Oh … so you were found under a cabbage leaf, adopted by Darth Vader, and raised by fairies?"

He smoothed out the wrinkles on his trousers with hands as big as an iron. "Where did you get fairies from?"

"Something sweet had to be involved in your upbringing. Why not fairies? You have shown me a moment or two when I'm sure you weren't raised by wolves." I saw the attendant approach with her cart, and I released Mark's tray and then mine to prepare for our free beverage.

"Can I get you something to drink?" That girl was definitely heading home to Dallas. Her Texas twang didn't allow her to be from any place else.

Mark looked at me, then back at the attendant. "We'll have two vodkas and orange juice." He pulled his credit card out of his wallet and handed it to the woman, who was all too happy to stand there and smile at him.

"We're drinking this early?"

He looked at his watch. "It's just past noon, and if you're going to ask me personal questions throughout the flight, I'm going to need a drink."

Most times I wanted to hug this man, but right now I wanted to slug him.

A minute later, the flight attendant plopped two bags of pretzels and our drinks on the tray. "Let me know if you need anything else, sugar." She gave him a mile-high-club smile and rolled her cart away.

"Does that happen all the time to you?"

He opened the tiny vodka bottles and poured it into the orange juice, then passed the first drink to me.

"Does what happen?"

"Women tripping over their knickers to be close to you."

"You're imagining things."

"You are definitely getting an eye exam when we get home." I leaned across his lap to make sure the attendant wasn't standing in the hallway behind us. "She gave you that come-hither, I-want-to-bang-you-in-the-bathroom look."

When I pulled back, he leaned into the aisle to have a look. "I didn't notice."

I took a sip of my drink. The taste of vodka sent a shiver down my spine. "How could you not notice? She practically stirred your orange juice with her nipple." I slapped my hand over my mouth.

Mark laughed a full belly laugh. "What happened to Jess Stone, my assistant?"

"I'm sorry. It's been a stressful morning, and I lose my filter when I lose my patience."

He took a long minute digesting my statement. His lips curled up at the corners until his perfectly straight smile threatened to melt my insides. "I like this Jess."

I took another swig of my drink. "You don't like the normal Jess?" My heart squeezed enough to cause me chest pain. Here I'd been trying to keep it professional at the office, and it turned out that my boss didn't even like me.

"I like you, Jess. All the facets of you. I like you too much for my own good." He drained his doctored orange juice and hit the call button for the attendant, who wasted no time rushing back to him.

"Two more, please."

I sat in contemplative silence. Did my boss just tell me he liked me? As in *like me* liked me? What did *too much for his own good* mean?

I turned in my seat to face him. "Now that you have one down, you should be numbed up enough to deal with my questions."

The attendant brought two more, only this time she opened the bottles and poured them into the drinks. "Where you headed?"

I wanted to laugh because we were trapped on a plane to Dallas.

"Aspen," Mark said in a friendly enough tone.

"Oh, the weather in Colorado is brutal right now. I've a got a friend grounded in Denver." She leaned against his chair, pressing her thigh against Mark's shoulder.

"That's too bad." Mark turned his body away from her and handed me one of the two drinks.

I looked up to watch the smile fall from the attendant's face. Yep, she'd definitely hoped for something more out of Mark, based on how sullenly she walked away after his dismissal. "Do you think this is wise?" I brought the remainder of the first drink to my lips and emptied the cup.

"We've got hours of travel. Wise? Probably not, but sometimes we just have to put ourselves out there and see what happens."

I lifted the second cup and waited for him to do the same. "To the unwise moments that make our lives more exciting." We tapped plastic glasses and took a drink. "Now, where were we?"

"You were in full-fledged interrogation mode."

The first drink was already hitting, and I felt lightheaded and giddy. "I was just beginning. I haven't even reached for my spotlight or the pliers to tear out your fingernails."

"Harsh. And I was thinking you just wanted to know about my family."

I relaxed into the seat. "I want to know everything about you. I have since the day I met you." I let my hair fall over my face to cover the heated blush I knew was blooming on my cheeks.

He brushed my hair aside and tucked it behind my ear. "All you had to do was ask, Jess. I'd tell you anything."

CHAPTER FIVE

MARK

What the hell am I doing? Jess looked up at me with those big eyes that managed to see right through me.

"You'd tell me anything?"

I considered her question. Her skepticism was warranted; I hadn't exactly been the most public person during our time working together. "I'll make you a deal. What's said at thirty thousand feet stays at thirty thousand feet. There's also one caveat, and that's you have to answer a question for every one you ask."

She twisted her long hair around her finger and left it hanging in a spiral over her shoulder. "Okay. Who goes first?"

"You're the curious one." That wasn't entirely true. I wanted to know everything about her, but I knew it wasn't wise. The more time I spent with Jess, the more I wanted. My world was filled with hostility, and she was my one guilty pleasure, even if only from afar.

"Tell me about your father."

I turned as much as a giant could turn in an economy seat. My torso twisted toward her; my legs lifted the tray, almost upending my open pretzels and drink. Jess moved my things to her tray. She closed mine, giving me more room. I didn't deserve her, but I was glad I had her. On a crappy day like today, she was the best person to have by my side. She's the best assistant I've had. Not to mention the cutest. "That's more than a question. It's more like a therapy session."

She twisted her body until her knee came to rest against my leg. "Okay, so was he always mean?"

That was a hard question to answer because *mean* wasn't the right word. "Not mean, just unapproachable. My father was an iceberg. His life was spent conquering the world."

Jess sighed and laid her hand on my arm. "I'm sorry to hear that. What's your life goal?"

That was easy. "I want to conquer my father." I sipped my drink and laid my head back. The alcohol was starting to have the desired calming effect. "That was two questions."

"You're right. It's your turn." She pulled her trouser-clad legs into the seat and curled into a compact little ball.

"Are you close to your family?" Her hair fell in front of her face again, and I itched to push it aside. She had the greenest eyes. They were the color of dark moss, and their pairing with her chestnut hair and pale skin made her stunning. With a quick swipe and tuck, I uncovered eyes that bewitched me. One look from her and I was ready to give her anything.

"Yes," she said without thought, then started to bob her head from shoulder to shoulder. "Well, I'm close to my parents. As

35

for my sister … how close would you want to come to a rabid dog?"

I sipped my drink and chuckled. Jess rarely had a cross word to say about anyone. Hearing her describe her sister as a contagious mutt was funny. "Sounds dangerous."

"She has a fierce bark and bite. She's two years older … and she hates me."

My back stiffened at her comment. It was impossible to hate this woman. "She's just jealous."

Jess sat up straight. "Of what? She has everything. She married a doctor. Lives in a big beautiful house in Connecticut. She has a son, a housekeeper, a gardener, and a nanny. She drives a Range Rover and wears Chanel. Her teeth are capped, her hair is cut by Jennifer Aniston's stylist, and she gets a colonic every quarter." She collapsed against the seat like listing her sister's accomplishments was exhausting.

"And that's a good thing?"

"Everything but the colonic. That sounds awful." She picked up her half-full cup and drained it.

I wanted to laugh; instead, I leaned my head into the aisle to get the flight attendant's attention and signaled for two more drinks.

"Those are just things. I bet she doesn't have your smile or your beautiful green eyes or your sense of humor. I bet her lips aren't full and kissable. I bet her body isn't curved like an hourglass. She certainly doesn't smell like sunshine or sound like a song when she speaks." I leaned forward until my lips were an inch from hers. "You are those things, Jess. Only you."

Her clouded eyes were filled with drink and desire. A desire I knew too well when I was alone with this woman. "Why do you have to be my boss? Why can't you just be a man?"

Why indeed? What was I thinking bringing her on this trip? *I need her with me.* That was what I was thinking. This merger was a big deal to me, and I didn't have anyone to share it with. Not true, exactly—I didn't have anyone I wanted to share it with but Jess.

I leaned back just as the flight attendant delivered our drinks. This time she didn't stay to chat. "Drink up, beautiful. We've got a long day ahead of us."

I turned back to face the seat in front of me. Any closer to Jess and I'd be kissing her senseless. I had to ask myself if that was wise.

She finished off her drink and closed her eyes. Fifteen minutes into her sleep she snuggled over and laid her head on my shoulder. I knew I should push her back, but it felt too perfect. And when she set her hand on my chest, I was in heaven.

I pressed my chair back and closed my eyes. My hand covered hers, and for the first and only time ever, Jess Stone and I slept together.

When the captain's voice came on over the loudspeaker, we both jolted awake. I looked at her, and she returned my gaze, but we both remained silent. We brought our seats to the upright position and prepared for the landing. She white-knuckled the handle again, but I didn't dare offer her comfort this time. I only had a modicum of professionalism left inside me, and one more touch of Jess would erase it all.

We bolted from the plane and raced to the next gate where our flight was loading. This time our seats were separated. I was both relieved and disappointed. She was sitting three seats behind me and across the aisle. I busied myself getting ready for tomorrow's meeting. I tried not to look at her, but each time I chanced a glance back, our eyes connected.

Just over two hours later, we landed in Cheyenne, Wyoming.

The sky was dark and cloudy with flurries of snow blowing around the planes. A light dusting of white covered the ground.

"We need to hurry," she said. Her boots clicked across the cement floor of the concourse. She raced toward the rental cars. "Hello," she said in a voice that didn't give away our three-drink binge hours ago. "I have a reservation under Cantwell."

The desk clerk looked up the name. "There's a slight problem."

Jess shifted her eyes from the clerk, to me, then back to the clerk. "What problem?"

"The car you reserved hasn't been turned back in."

Jess pressed her fingers to her temples and rubbed.

I lifted my brow and stared at the clerk. "And?"

The woman's fingers skated across the keys. "And I have a replacement, but it's a front-wheel drive and not a four-wheel drive."

"We'll take it." My voice was gruff enough to get her fingers moving across the keyboard at a lightning pace.

"Wait," Jess said. "A front-wheel drive is not going to be enough for this weather." She pointed outside to where the snow had turned from flurries to big floating flakes. "We need a four-wheel drive."

The clerk smiled a piss-off smile. "You may need a four-wheel drive, but we don't have one. There's the Honda Accord or the Ford Mustang."

I looked at the line behind us and said, "We'll take the Accord."

"Full-coverage insurance?"

"No," I said.

"Yes," Jess said. "In this weather, we may need it. And I'll drive." She dug in her purse for what I imagined was her driver's license.

I slid my credit card across the counter with my driver's license. Not wanting to argue any further, I agreed to the insurance, but not her offer to drive. Fifteen minutes later, we were on our way.

"Do you always purchase extra insurance?" The wipers of the silver Accord swished back and forth with little effect. I hiked up the fan of the defroster and waited for the ice coating the windshield to melt.

"No, but we're entering a lousy storm with a substandard car. You should have let me drive. I'm from snow country."

"While I appreciate the offer, I need to drive. It keeps my mind busy." *It keeps my mind off of wanting to kiss you*, I wanted to add but didn't.

"Fine, but the insurance was necessary. Both of us drank hours ago, and we're tired. We're not drunk anymore, but if your reflexes are like mine, they are bit slower than usual. I thought we'd be better safe and not sorry." She wrapped her jacket around her shoulders and shivered.

"You cold?" I reached for the controls to switch the heat from defroster to the dash.

"Leave it on defrost. I'm fine."

We sat in silence for a few minutes before Jess asked, "When was the last time you saw your father?"

That was an easy one. "Ten years ago at my mother's funeral."

"Oh." She turned toward the fogged-up window and slid her hand from under the jacket long enough to wipe it down. "I'm sorry, Mark."

"Oh, don't be. I didn't know her. She had worked for my dad, and when she gave birth to me, she left as soon as the wet nurse showed up."

Her hand came to rest on my arm. "But you went to her funeral?"

"I thought it only right since she was my mother. What about you? When was the last time you saw your parents?"

"Last year at Christmas. We all meet up in Colorado to catch up every year."

"So that's why the holidays are so important to you?" I reached up to feel the air coming out of the defroster; it was as cold as the air outside. No wonder it wasn't doing a great job clearing the glass.

"Yes, I guess. I like the tradition, but I love Christmas. I love the decorations and the music." She reached down and turned on the radio. Some song called *Santa Baby* filled the car. "I love eggnog and wrapping paper and candy canes and ornaments. I love that it's a time to reflect on the past and plan for the future. It's a time to enjoy the ones you love and tolerate the ones you can barely stand."

"Like your sister?"

"Exactly." She fiddled with the defroster button, and the window cleared. "It was on the blue."

"Details. That's why I need you, Jess. You're the best at the details."

"I do what I can. Now tell me why you don't like the holidays."

I shrugged. I couldn't pinpoint anything exactly. "Maybe it's because we never celebrated Christmas as such. We were usually on the road when I was a kid. There was always some contract to negotiate. I've only had a Christmas tree once in my life, and that was because a girl I was seeing in college set one up in my dorm room as a surprise."

"Was it a nice surprise?"

"Sure, but I enjoyed her little elf costume more than the tree."

"You're a man. It's to be expected." She fidgeted in her seat. "Do you have a girlfriend now? Someone who is wishing you were going to be home for Christmas?"

Was that wistfulness I caught in her voice? "No, I'm not seeing anyone. I'm pretty much married to my work."

"So it would seem the apple doesn't fall far from the tree."

Wounded by her words, I turned my head toward her for just a second, but it was the exact second I hit a patch of black ice.

The car slid across the lanes, and no matter which way I turned the steering wheel, it wasn't right. We spun in a circle twice, then slid into a bank of snow piled high on the shoulder of the highway. The car died, the snow fell around us, and everything went silent.

CHAPTER SIX

JESS

"Are you okay?" Mark's hands were all over my body, checking for injuries.

I rubbed the knot forming on my forehead from the knock against the glass. "Yes, I'm fine. You?" I turned in my seat to look at him. He seemed fine except for the loss of color in his face. "Are you okay, Mark?"

He rubbed his face with his palm. "Fine. I'm fine. Just shocked, is all. I wasn't expecting that."

I started to laugh. I wasn't sure if it was shock or what, but I laughed and laughed until my stomach hurt. "I bet you're glad I forced that full-coverage insurance on you now, aren't you?"

He stared at me blankly. It took a minute for him to catch up, and then he was laughing too. "Always looking out for me. Maybe you should have driven too." He stared at my forehead. "You did get hurt. I can see the bump rising on your head."

I touched the tender area with my fingers. "I've had worse. Remember, I'm a younger sister."

He unbuckled his seatbelt. "I hope I never run into your sister. She sounds awful."

"You'd probably like her. She has a kind of charm that most men find attractive."

"I'm not like most men, Jess." He shut the engine off and then tried to start it again, but it didn't turn over. It spit and sputtered, then coughed and died. He pulled his phone from his pocket. "No signal." Mark took the sleeve of his jacket and wiped at the iciness coating the inside of the window. "Let's see what we have in store for us."

He opened the door and stepped out, but his leather-soled Italian loafers didn't give much purchase, and he fell to his fine ass.

"Damn it." He slipped and slid on the icy ground and finally found a piece of ground where he could get a grip.

I grabbed the handle of my door and pushed, but it went nowhere. We were safely embedded in a snowbank.

"Perfect," I heard him say, which meant our situation was anything but.

I reached into the glove compartment, took out the map, and then crawled across the seat to exit. I plopped out on the other side. I didn't fall because I wore appropriate shoes. My Geox boots were both stylish and practical. I closed my jacket up around my neck and shivered as the snow whipped around us.

No one was on the road. No one would come to our rescue because no one was crazy enough to go out in this storm. I pressed the map onto the drivers-side seat and took a look at where we were. The last mile marker had said we were thirty miles inside the state of Colorado.

"There's a gas station up ahead about a mile." I pointed to the little blue indicator on the map.

"Get back in the car, Jess, it's cold out here. I got us into this mess, I'll get us out." He pulled his suit jacket tight in front of him.

"Where's your coat?"

"I didn't bring one. I thought we'd get off the plane and right into a taxi. I'd get the deal signed. I'd put you in a car and myself back on the next flight home."

"What am I going to do with you?" I pried open the back door and pulled my suitcase close.

"What are you doing?"

"I'm saving your life." I opened my suitcase and pulled out three wrapped packages. I tore open the beautiful paper and pulled a sweater free. "This was for my dad, but you need it more."

Mark shook his head. "I've got stuff in my bag."

"Really, like what? Another suit? Two finely pressed shirts? A pair of underwear and a selection of ties?"

I knew I'd hit the mark when his shoulders slumped. "I can layer what I have."

I reached up to touch the collar of his tie. "Custom fit doesn't leave much room for layering." I tugged at his suit jacket until he allowed me to remove it. "Put this on and then put your jacket back on if you can." He couldn't so he

45

put the jacket back on, then pulled the sweater over his suit.

Next, I opened the gift for my mom. It was a scarf and hat. Beige cable-knit with heavy fringe. "It will do in a pinch." I pulled the hat over his red ears and wrapped the scarf around his neck.

His shaking from the cold slowed. "I'll replace these as soon as we get to Aspen. There are plenty of shops there."

I didn't want to tell him these were special and couldn't be replaced. That I'd knitted the hat and scarf myself, and that I'd scoured every store to find the perfect color sweater to match my dad's brown eyes. So instead, I said, "Don't worry. I have more presents in my bag."

It was true. I had lots of little trinkets from movies for Ben, to my sister's stationery, to gift cards and framed pictures for my parents. "Besides, it's not about the gift, it's about the experience," I continued. "You should try an old-fashioned Christmas some day."

I closed the back door and walked to the front to get my purse and pull the keys from the ignition. Once I had the keys in my hand, I locked the door and shut it.

"Where do you think you're going? I said I'd get us help."

I shook my head too hard and winced at the pain it caused. "I'm not staying here. I probably have a concussion, and I'd fall asleep and die before you ever came back." I meant it as a joke, but the way his face fell told me he took my head injury seriously.

"Jess, you should really stay here with the car. Someone might come to help."

We both looked at the car buried in the embankment and then out toward the deserted highway.

"No one is coming, Mark. Let's go."

"We shouldn't leave our things in the car. Someone could steal them," he said as I pulled him farther from the car.

Once again I looked at the deserted highway. "Who is going to steal our things?"

He tucked his hands into his pant pockets and hunched forward into the wind. "I'm sorry about this, Jess."

I nudged against him. "It's never a dull moment with you."

It was an arduous mile-long walk to the gas station. By the time we arrived at what turned out to be a sleepy truck stop, both Mark and I were human popsicles.

He walked straight to the coffee pot and poured himself a jumbo cup. I opted for hot chocolate with an extra dose of whipped topping. Mark paid and asked the clerk where we could find a tow truck.

There was silence followed by laughter. "Dude, even the tow trucks don't want to be out in this shit. Have you seen the forecast?"

"I've got money, lots of it. Find me a tow truck driver and I'll give you a hundred bucks. Find me one in the next fifteen minutes and I'll give you five hundred."

The kid got right on the phone.

Mark turned toward me and brushed off the melting snow that had accumulated on my hood and shoulders. "I'm really sorry, Jess." He walked me to where hot dogs were turning on the grill. "It's not the meal I was thinking we'd have, but it will do for now." He pressed two dogs in two buns and went from condiment to condiment asking me what I wanted.

When he had my chili-dog made perfectly, he walked me over to a nearby table before going to the register to pay. When he returned, he had a bag of various candy bars and packages of donuts and a jumbo bag of Doritos—Cool Ranch, the kind I liked best.

"Tow trucks on its way."

I took too big of a bite and felt the chili ooze out the corner of my lip. Before I could respond, Mark swiped his finger across it and stuck it in his mouth. "I was wrong to put sauerkraut on mine."

"I'll share." I offered my hot dog to him, and he took a bite. From that point forward, we shared the whole meal. Ten minutes later, a grizzled old man with bad teeth and a worse attitude approached.

"You the one with the money and a car problem?"

Mark wiped his mouth and hands with a napkin and stood. He towered over the man. Even so, the old curmudgeonly man stood his ground.

"Yes, we slid off the road about a mile down. We could really use your help."

He looked at Mark from his cable-knit cap all the way to his fine leather shoes. "It'll cost ya."

Mark shook his head. "There was no doubt in my mind."

"Gather your girl and let's go."

"She's staying here while we go."

"I am not," I chimed in. "I'm going with you."

WRAPPED AROUND MY HEART

"Jess, please. I'd feel better if you stayed."

I looked around the place for emphasis. At most of the booths were men—alone—staring at me. "I'd feel better if I went." I gathered our snacks and shoved them back into the plastic sack.

"You two lovers want to stay and quarrel or do you want to get your car out of the ditch and be on your way?"

Mark let out a huff. "Let's go." He slid the cashier a wad of bills on our way out.

The old man was two steps ahead of us, but his voice was loud and clear. "Giving in is always better, son. You may win the fight, but with most women, you'll lose the war."

"It's not like that with us," Mark replied. He helped me into the heated cab of the tow truck.

"That's what you think now." The old man forced his truck into gear and we were rolling.

It was a short drive to the car, but when we arrived, there was one big surprise I didn't expect. The back passenger window was busted out, and all of our things were gone.

CHAPTER SEVEN

MARK

The bastards took everything but my briefcase, which had somehow gotten lodged under Jess's seat during the crash.

Jess stood in a pile of broken glass with a look of disbelief frozen on her face. The gray sky blended in with her ashen skin.

The tow truck operator hooked a winch to the bumper. A low whine worked its way to a high-pitched squeal as the car was eased out of the snowbank.

There appeared to be little damage except for the post-accident shattered glass and a long thick scratch that ran the entire length of the passenger side of the car.

"I'll replace everything, Jess. I promise."

She turned toward me and laughed. "It's impossible. You can never replace the time and thought it took to decide on those gifts." She looked so deflated. Her hair hung limply around her shoulders. Her forehead sprouted a bruise where the knot had been, and her once pristine black trousers were now dotted with the salty stains of walking through a mile of slush.

One thing I knew for certain was that Jess Stone was not your average woman. Average would have cried the moment the car skidded. Average would have broken out into hysteria the minute the car crashed. Average wouldn't have come on this trip.

No ... Jess wasn't average, and every day I spent with her made me appreciate her more. It was in that instant that I knew I'd never be able to find another Jess Stone, and I'd do whatever it took to keep her.

"Should we call the police and file a report?"

She turned toward me and lifted her chin up to look into my eyes. "No," she said with determination. "We have to get going." She looked up to the sky. "It looks like we have a little reprieve from the snow."

"Get in your car and see if she'll start," the driver said just after he kicked the tailpipe, dislodging a clump of snow. "Usually it's just an air-exchange thing."

I carefully swiped at the bits of broken glass that had fallen on the driver's seat. Once inside, I gave the key a turn and listened as the car sputtered to life and then died.

"Give it some gas," the old man said.

I pumped the gas pedal twice and turned the key again. It coughed and sputtered, then purred to life. Pulling a few hundred from my wallet, I folded them into the tow truck driver's hand and helped Jess into the car.

We made it to the truck stop, knowing that an open window in the middle of a storm would never do. While Jess waited inside the car, hunched in front of the heating vent, I went in to get fleeced by the clerk for another twenty dollars. I picked up tape and plastic and a small plastic snow globe for Jess, hoping she'd see the humor in the gesture.

Lucky for us, we were between two storm bands, and the next hour was blizzard free.

"How's the head?" Each time I glanced over and saw Jess ready to fall asleep, I engaged her in conversation. I was worried sick that she'd fall asleep and I wouldn't be able to rouse her.

"It's fine. Nothing that a good night's sleep and a few layers of makeup can't resolve." Gripped tight in her palm was the snow globe. "I can't believe you bought me this." She shook it and watched the white flakes gather on the mountain peak.

"You seem like a nostalgic girl."

"And you want me to remember the time we went to Colorado together and you crashed the car on black ice?"

I reached over and placed my hand over hers. "I want you to look at this trip and know that it can't ever get worse than that moment."

"It won't take much effort to make it better. All we'd have to avoid is a crash and a robbery and it would be magical."

"I'll endeavor to make the rest of the trip magical."

"I'd like to see what that looks like."

"I'm going to show you magical, Jess, so you never have to question it when you see it." And that was what I set out to do. This wasn't a white carriage drawn by elegant horses, but the broken window did lend itself to the outdoorsy feel. I kept her awake with senseless chatter and fed her a bag full of carbohydrates.

We drove the next hour and a half without issue until whipping winds gradually blew the magic away into a whiteout.

"Pull in over there." Jess pointed to the red neon sign above the gas station. "It's the last stop before we go through the pass."

While I pumped the gas, she went inside to grab coffee. When she emerged, her complexion was the color of snow.

"What's wrong?" I rushed to her side and cupped her face with my hands. "Are you feeling sick or dizzy?"

She leaned into my hand. "This is getting less magical the farther we get along." She looked back toward the store. "The pass is closed."

I dropped my hand and whipped around to look down the highway. Sure enough, the snow gates were lowering. Red flashing lights illuminated a *road closed* sign.

"Damnit." I wrapped my arm around her shoulder and walked her into the store, where it was at least warmer than it was outside.

"What are we going to do?"

If I hadn't already suspected it, this confirmed that Jess wasn't feeling her best—because she was never without ideas, this question was totally out of character. Normally she'd say, "This is what we're going to do." It was my turn to step up and take charge.

"Go grab some snacks, and I'll figure something out." I skipped the clerk because he was a kid, and I went directly to a robust trucker piling relish on a dog. "Do you think the pass will open back up tonight?"

Although he had a Santa Claus face, he delivered a Grinch message. "Nope. The whole side of the hill came down on the highway. It'll take hours for the road crews to clean that up." He pointed to the television hanging above the register which showed the breaking news. "I'd bunk up for the night. If you ain't got a place, I'd hurry and find one before they're all taken. There's a motel one block down and one over. It's not much, but it's clean."

I swiped a few toothbrushes off the shelf and went in search of Jess, whom I found debating between powdered-sugar and chocolate-covered donuts. "Grab both and anything else you might want. Looks like we're stuck for the night."

Her head snapped up. "Are you kidding me?"

"Not a chance. You know me, I don't kid. Let's go." I paid, and we hopped in the beat-up Accord toward the only place I knew existed for lodging.

Pine Lodge was nothing to look at, but given the alternative —sleeping in the drafty car—it looked downright five-star. "I'll get each of us a room. Stay here." I was out of the car before she could argue.

The front-desk clerk looked like he'd just walked off the set of a B movie: clueless, out-of-touch, likely to smoke his lunch and drink his dinner. So, basically, he fit in perfectly with the shabby Pine Lodge.

"Good evening." It was close enough. The last of the light from the hidden sun was setting behind the peak, and a gray dismal day was turning to black.

"Yep. What can I do for ya?" He shuffled through the newspaper ads on his desk.

"I need two rooms, please."

His head was shaking back and forth before I even finished my sentence. "No can do."

I pulled my wallet out of my pocket and laid it on the counter. The corner of a crisp bill from my recent ATM withdrawal peeked out of the fold.

"Surely you can." I pulled the bill from my wallet and pressed it across the counter. It was only a twenty, though I was willing to pay anything to get Jess into a room.

"I don't have two rooms. I've got one."

"Please tell me it has two beds."

The man took the twenty off the counter and pushed it inside the front pocket of his worn-out jeans. "I can tell you it has two beds, but I don't much like to lie."

The bell on the door rang, and another stranded person walked in, looking hopeful.

"I'll take it." I was a businessman, and I knew when I'd been offered the best deal. A one bedroom was it today.

When I got back out to the car with our room key, Jess was leaning against the window, drawing circles in the ice that formed inside the glass. She turned around, and even in the twilight, her eyes were like sparkling gemstones.

"I have good news and bad news." I put the car in reverse and pulled it to the end of the building.

"No more bad news. I can't handle anything more."

I parked and rushed around to open her door. Under the bright streetlights, I could see the damage from the crash was more significant than I'd originally thought. The whole panel was flattened.

"Good news it is." I reached past her to grab the bag of sweets and my briefcase. "We got a room."

"Oh, thank goodness. I was worried that with all the cars in the lot, we wouldn't get rooms."

She followed me to room 134. I opened the door and let it swing wide. The Ritz it wasn't, but it was clean, and there was a bed.

"What room number are you in?" She walked past me and snatched the key from my hand.

I looked at the door. "That's the bad news. There was only one room left."

She looked at me. Looked at the bed. Looked back at me. "No. This will never work. I'm not sleeping with my boss."

CHAPTER EIGHT

JESS

O
h lord. What the hell was I supposed to do? I'd
fantasized about getting Mark in bed at least a thousand times, but this wasn't how I'd envisioned it going down.

"You couldn't come up with one more room?" I stared at the bed. It wasn't even king-sized. "You are the master negotiator. What happened in there?" Did he hear the panic in my voice? Was it written all over my face?

"You can't get what's not available, sweetheart. I did the best I could." He closed the door and walked inside. Mark was a big man, and his presence swallowed up the room.

"I'm sorry." I plopped down on the bed. "It's just been a crazy day." My fingers went to the bump on my forehead.

"Does it still hurt?" He stood in front of me and took a knee. Deft fingers unzipped my boots and tugged them off. His warm hands rubbed at my cold sock-covered toes.

"If I say yes, will you continue to rub my feet?" He was so close. I trapped my hands under my thighs so I didn't reach out and thread my fingers through his hair.

"I'll rub your feet for as long as you need me to." He moved from my toes up the sensitive arch and settled his palms around my ankles. "What you really need is a hot shower and a couple of aspirin."

"You're probably right, but I appreciate the foot rub, none-theless." I rose from the bed, making him scoot back to allow me room. I discarded my jacket and tossed it over the worn wooden desk chair.

"How about you take a shower, and I go find a bottle of wine? Maybe a glass will help you relax and fall asleep." He stood up and walked to the door.

"That sounds good." I looked down at my black slacks and my silk shirt. It was all I had. I'd worn it all day, and it looked like I'd wear it all night. "If you're going back to the truck stop, can you see if they have a something I can wear to bed besides this?"

He nodded before he walked out.

My first task was to call my parents. I hadn't let them know of the change of plans. I figured I'd call them when I got to Aspen but seeing as I hadn't made it to Aspen ...

The phone rang three times before my mom answered. "Are you almost there? I've been worried sick about you. The storm is crazy, and the roads are a mess."

"Hi, Mom." Most conversations started with a greeting.

"Oh, I'm sorry, honey. I was so worried I forgot the pleas-antries. How are you? Where are you?"

I pulled out the chair and sat. "There's been a glitch in my plans." I had called last night and told them I'd be a day late, but now I wasn't sure I'd make it at all. If the weather didn't let up, I might be stuck here for days. "The weather has been a problem." I explained about our flight changes, the car accident, and now the pass closure.

"I'm not sure if I want to hate your boss or love him."

"You can do both. He's big enough to take it all."

"You're safe, right?"

"I am. Mark got a room, and as soon as I hang up, I'm taking a shower and crawling between the sheets to watch meaningless television."

"Wait … did you say a room, or he got you your room?" Mom was a librarian and a detail person.

"He got the only room left."

"Two beds?"

I gave her a moment of library silence. "It's not ideal, but it will work out all right."

"Well, he can sleep on the couch." Mom was matter-of-fact. "He's already inconvenienced you enough. I know you, Jess, and it's like you to give up the bed. Don't."

I looked around the room, which had a bed, a stained turquoise colored chair in the corner, and a desk and chair against the wall. Mom was used to higher-end lodging, but like Mark said, *You can't get what's not available.* "We've got it worked out." We didn't, but she didn't need to know that.

She told me to keep her posted before we hung up.

59

The shower was basic, but it was hot. I stood under the stream and let the water wash away all the bad from the day. A tap sounded at the door, and I stuck my head out of the curtain.

"Is that you, Mark?"

He inched the door open and dropped a plastic bag on the floor. "I got what they had. It's not much, but it's clean."

"Thank you."

"Jess," he said from the crack in the door, "I'm really sorry about this."

"It's okay, it's not like you planned it."

He laughed. "Sweetheart, if this had been planned, you wouldn't be alone in that shower." He closed the door, leaving me with that vision in my head. And what was that comment supposed to mean?

Out of the shower, I towel-dried my body and my hair. When I opened the bag, I laughed. The T-shirt had already been unfolded, and the words *I Put Out for Santa* stood out in neon red against the white background.

"You're kidding me!" I called out. "That's all they had?"

His footsteps neared the bathroom door. "No, they had a rich assortment with sayings that ranged from *cock-a-doodle-do-me* to *pet my pussy*. That was the least offensive of the bunch."

"I can't imagine." I pulled out a pair of shorts that said *juicy* across the ass. "Really?" I cried out again.

"There were only two options in shorts. The ones I bought or ones with a dachshund on the back."

I slipped on the boxers and opened the door. Mark was leaning against the doorframe. Only he wasn't suited up anymore. His once pristinely pressed dress shirt was untucked, unbuttoned and hanging open. There was no question now about coffee putting hair on his chest. He was testosterone on overload.

Stunned for a second or maybe a full minute, I stared at the hair that begged to be touched. The accident hadn't killed me, but tonight would. I raised my hand to touch him but thought better of it and walked away.

"What was worse about the dachshund?"

"It said *I love wieners*. I can go back and get you those." He lifted a brow.

"Oh lord, what's wrong with people?"

He turned and leaned back against the wall. The shirt fell open farther, giving me a perfect vision of his broad chest and hard abs. My heart galloped up into my throat. What the hell was I going to do?

"I bought some stuff for dinner. It's not the Michelin-star restaurant I was looking forward to, but it will do." He walked into the bathroom and came out with two plastic cups. "I've opened the wine to let it breathe. Help yourself." He turned and shut the door.

When the water started, all I could think about was Mark Cantwell naked under the steamy stream.

Without hesitation, I poured a glass of the cheap red wine and turned on the television. Hoping to make a bad situation better, I rearranged the desk so we could sit on opposite sides.

I pulled up the two chairs we had—one the soiled fabric chair, the other a rickety wooden ladder-back.

I fan-folded a few Kleenexes and turned them into what almost resembled a flower and poked a pen through the bottom to make a stem.

I opened the bag to see what he had managed to bring and wrote the offerings down on a piece of notepaper, which I folded into a tent in front of his place setting.

With the menu in place, the flower on the table, and the food getting cold in the bag, I kicked back on the bed and waited. It wasn't star-rated cuisine, but at least it was better than a floor picnic.

Mark came out of the bathroom with wet hair and no shirt. The lower half of his body was covered in a pair of black sweatpants; his face, covered in amusement. Mark rarely smiled, but when he did, it was beautiful.

"You're amazing," he said, surveying my table setting. Much to my disappointment, he pulled on a T-shirt. On the front was a plumber with a speech bubble that read, *I'm Here to Lay Pipe*.

"Look at us." I looked at his shirt and then down at mine. It was too much to take in. I handed him a cup of wine. "Here's to a better tomorrow."

Mark shook his head and raised his glass. "At least you'll have a story to tell your parents when you make it home."

I hopped off the bed and walked toward the dining table. Mark's eyes followed my legs the entire time. Or was I concussed and imagining all his come-ons?

"About that. It's unlikely we'll make the ten o'clock meeting. Should I contact Mr. Braxton and reschedule?"

"I've already done that. He's willing to meet for dinner. Will you be okay staying the night tomorrow at the hotel? I'd feel better knowing that you're around should I need something."

I pulled out the wooden chair and sat down with a thunk. He took his place in the upholstered chair. It was a good decision because he sank so low he had dwindled to just a few inches above my height.

"Best decision I made all day," I said, looking at where the table pressed against his chest. "If I'd sat there, I would have had to scoop my food from the surface to my mouth."

Mark reached for the wine and topped off my glass. "I hope you like the red. It was the most expensive at $9.99 a bottle. Only the best for you." He shook out a paper napkin and placed it on his lap.

I leaned forward and pushed the menu toward him. "What would you like tonight?"

He looked up from the makeshift menu and ate me up with his eyes. Maybe under the dessert selections, I should have put my name. Too much wine gave me impure thoughts. Oh, who was I kidding; too much Mark gave me impure thoughts.

"I can't believe you made a menu."

I lifted my shoulders in a shrug. "We got lemons. I make lemonade."

He looked down at the menu and said, "I'll take the deep-fried burrito and a side of cold fries."

"Excellent choice." I reached for the bag and laid out his meal. I put the chicken sandwich and bag of chips in front of me. "Enjoy your meal."

We ate in silence until Mark spoke up. "You get another day of bonus pay. Will that help ease the pain of this disastrous trip?"

"I can't say the money won't help." I sipped at the wine, already feeling a little tipsy. "My sister bought my parents a cruise and then told me I owed her for half."

His jaw dropped. "I'm telling you. I hope I never have to meet your sister. She sounds like a piece of work."

I rolled my eyes. "Oh yeah, a real masterpiece."

"If you were home now, what would you be doing?" He dabbed at his lips like his napkin was cloth and we were in a fine restaurant.

"My home or my parents' home?" I took a bite of the sandwich. It wasn't bad for sitting in a warmer for hours and then cooling in the room for the past thirty minutes.

"Both." He leaned back, making the white T-shirt stretch across his chest. The damn man was distracting me.

"At my parents', I'd be making cookies instead of staring at your chest." I quickly covered my mouth with my hand. "Damn wine. No filter."

He picked up the bottle and poured me some more. "I like you when your guard is down. Drink up."

"At home, I'd be curled up in the corner of my couch watching some mindless television."

"Let's make ourselves at home." He scooted the chair back and walked to the bed where he made himself comfy leaning against the headboard. He turned on the television and scrolled through the stations while I finished my sandwich and chips.

"I called my mom when you were in the shower, and she said you have to sleep on the couch." With the bottle of wine in one hand and my cup in the other, I walked my *juicy*-emblazoned ass over to the bed and climbed on top of the comforter next to him.

CHAPTER NINE

JESS

"Did you tell your mom we didn't have a couch?"

"No. I just let her think my virtue was safe and would remain intact." I pulled my plastic cup to my lips and took a long drink. My thoughts were not far from Mark and what it would be like to sleep with him. He was a detail man. Someone who stopped at nothing to get what he wanted. Oh, to be wanted in that way by him. A girl could dream.

"Your virtue? You're not a …" He cocked his head like a confused kid. "… virgin, are you?"

I pointed down at my shirt. "No, I put out for Santa."

He laughed. "You know, a little-known secret is my middle name is Santa." His laugh was so robust that it shook the bed and upended my cup, which landed on his chest, sending red wine soaking into the white cotton.

"Oh. My. God. I'm so sorry." Without thinking, I straddled the man and started to pull his shirt up and off his body. "Mark, I'm so sorry." Once it was past his head, I went to work on dabbing the red liquid from his skin. "I'd fantasized about what you looked like naked, but it never happened with me dumping cheap wine on you." Realizing that I'd just had another non-filter moment, I pulled the stained shirt to my face. "God, did I say that?"

His hands wrapped around my wrists and pulled the shirt down from my face. I was certain the color of my cheeks matched the scarlet wine now soaked into his shirt.

Those damn bedroom eyes stared back at me. A sexy-as-sin smile lifted the edges of his lips. "You said it. Did you mean it?"

I squirmed and prepared to crawl off his lap. This day was going from bad to worse in a heartbeat.

He let go of my wrists and gripped my hips, holding me in place.

I chewed my inner cheek, wondering how I should answer. There wasn't a right answer; there was only the truth. But was I brave enough or tipsy enough to be honest?

My head fell forward, and my hair created a curtain to hide my embarrassment. "To be honest, I have a crush on you. I know it's not right, and it's not professional, but it is what it is."

While one hand kept me locked in place, the other hand reached up to move my hair aside. He lifted my chin, so I was forced to look at him. "You have a crush on me?" There was a softness in his eyes that I'd never seen before.

I nodded. "Guilty."

One hand cupped my cheek, and his thumb brushed across my lower lip. He lifted his body so his beautiful chest was touching me and his lips were a breath from mine.

"So I haven't been the only one suffering?" His fingers ran down my cheek to my neck to my shoulder and back to my hip.

"What do you mean?"

His fingers skated up and down from my waist to my ribs over and over again. Gooseflesh rose on my skin.

"The best part of my day is when I pick up my coffee because I get to touch you for the briefest of moments. The second-best part is when it's just you and me in the office planning for the day."

All the air left my lungs. "You like me?"

"I more than like you, Jess. I've been lusting after you since the day I hired you."

"You have?" I leaned forward until my T-shirt-covered breasts grazed his bare chest.

"Yes." He pushed forward until his lips gently touched mine. "This isn't wise, but it's probably inevitable."

"Probably," I said as I pressed my mouth firmly against his. The heat of his kiss raked down my spine.

His lips parted, and his tongue probed at the crease of mine until I gave way to his persistence and kissed him deeply. With slow precision, he explored my mouth. Soft velvet slid against my tongue in a give and take that made my stomach flip and flop.

His hands wrapped around my back and pulled me close—so close that I could feel his heart race to catch up with the pace of mine.

We spent minutes in our first kiss until we parted to catch a breath.

"Amazing. So much more than I anticipated."

My brain was muddled, and I was only capable of single-word responses. "More?"

"Oh, Jess, you taste like …"

"Wine and stupidity?"

He reached up and cupped my cheeks. "No. You taste like sugar and spice and sex all rolled into one hot little package."

"But what about work?" I had no idea what kissing Mark meant for my job. "I just kissed my boss."

That smile I loved spread wide across his face. "Your boss isn't here. It's just me, Mark the man, with a woman I've been hot after for almost a year. A woman who leaves the room and takes the light with her each time she goes."

Those words caused heat to rush through my veins and stall in my core until I was a throbbing mess of need. "What about tomorrow?"

His erection pulsed between my thighs. "What's the elevation here?"

Thrown by his question and the ever-growing rod pressed against the cotton of my shorts, I was silenced. Seconds later I had enough cells working to process another word. "Elevation?"

"It's got to be about eight thousand feet." He lifted his hips and pressed his hardness against me. "What happens here stays here, just like the plane."

"I'm beginning to like high altitude. I just wonder if it's messed with the logical sides of our brains." Without conscious thought, I ground my hips into his lap.

"You're an amazing assistant, and I can't live without you in the office." He peppered my lips with quick soft kisses. "I'm pretty sure I can't live without you in my bed right now either. Say no and I'll sleep on the floor and make your mom happy. Say yes and I'll give you a night you'll never forget. What do you say, Jess?"

He wanted sex with me. I had never been so excited or scared in my life. "So this is a one-time, no-strings, no-repercussions, hot moment?"

He chuckled. "No, Jess, this is an all-night, get-our-fill, let's-see-where-it-takes-us hot moment."

My chest vibrated with my laugh. "Well, as long as you promise it will be hot, I'm all in." I slid my fingers through the hair on his chest, and when I breezed past his nipples, he hissed.

"Who knew that today would turn out to be awesome after all?" He gripped the hem of my T-shirt and pulled it over my head, leaving both of us bare from the waist up. "God, you have beautiful breasts."

My painfully hard nipples pointed straight at him. He pulled me tight to his groin where his rock-hard length sat in the cradle between my thighs.

His lips covered one nipple and drew it into the heat of his mouth. His teeth grazed the tender swollen peak, sending a jolt of desire through me. A moan ripped from my throat.

He pulled back and looked at me. "I love that sound. I want to hear that all night." He leaned in and worked on the other nipple until my throaty moans were a string of notes that never ended.

When his hand reached inside the waistband of the shorts, I gasped. This was really happening. I was nearly naked with Mark Cantwell, the man who made work worthwhile. The man whose very presence made the sun rise in my world. The man who would ultimately break my heart when this ended.

"What do you like?" His hand slid around the inside of the cotton underwear to knead my bottom.

"I don't know." I pressed forward to kiss him. It was a quick pass-by that needed to be longer because I knew this moment wouldn't last. This was a conditional coming together, based on a storm, a crash, and a closed highway. Without the debacles of the day, we'd never be in bed together. We'd be in Aspen drinking substandard coffee and analyzing a contract.

"I like you," I said in a whisper against his warm lips. His tongue parted my lips and dipped inside my mouth. It was like the softest velvet or the finest silk. A delicious treat to savor, not devour in a single serving.

He lifted me from his lap and laid me on the bed next to him, then covered me with his body. His weight pushed me into the mattress until he rose on his arms and looked down at me.

"You are simply the most beautiful woman," he whispered against my ear. "You have no idea how many times I wondered what was beneath your blouse, your skirt, your pants." He took in my body with a slow sweep of his eyes.

My fingers danced across his chest, over his shoulders, and down his back until my hands rested on the hard globes of solid steel buns. The man was ripped from head to toe. He shimmied down my body. His lips grazed and plucked at needy nipples. His mouth kissed and sucked at my skin until he reached the edge of my shorts. "Shall we see how juicy I can make you?"

A rolling shudder thundered down my spine to my sex. "Oh, god, yes." I lifted my hips as he tugged the material free. He didn't give me much time to prep for him. He spread my legs and buried his face into my folds. Long strokes had me lifting my hips off the bed to meet him. The sharp grate of his teeth across my sex made me hiss. The soft flattened strokes of his tongue soothed the sting. And when he slid one of his fingers deep inside me, my body quaked—little shivers of an almost orgasm—an explosion letting off a little pressure before the big bang.

"Feels so good," I whimpered as he pulled the bundle of raw nerves between his lips and sucked. My thighs shook. My stomach tightened. He filled my channel with another finger and thrust deep inside me. "Mark … I'm …"

He pulled his mouth away. "No, you're not. Not yet. The best things are better when you have to wait for them."

He slid back up my body and suckled my breasts. Two fingers turned into one. His touch slowed, and my body softened into the mattress.

"Take off your pants." I yanked and pulled at his waistband but only moved it inches.

"You want me naked?"

"Yes. I want you."

He rose from the bed and pulled the tie loose. The sweatpants dropped to his hips, giving me a perfect view of his stomach muscles, the perfect V, and a happy trail leading me to his full erection. He pulled the elastic waist over his erection.

"Holy shit."

Like the cocky man I knew him to be, he winked at me. "Can you handle it?"

I always loved a challenge, and although I'd never experienced something of that magnitude, I was game to try. "You know what they say: go big or go home."

He stepped out of his pants and crawled between my legs. "Birth control?"

I nodded. "Sex partners?"

He shook his head. "Not for a long time, sweetheart. I've been dreaming of you. Anyone or anything I should be concerned with?" His eyes were no longer blue but a steely gray that spoke of desire and passion.

"No one but you."

"You okay like this then?" He nudged at my entrance.

"This is perfect."

He pressed forward in one thrust, and I swore the heavens opened and the angels sang.

"You okay?"

"Yes, it's so good," I panted, trying to keep from falling off the cliff. So on edge was my body that the fullness caused a ripple to pulse through me. He held still until my sex stopped throbbing, and I adjusted to his size. His arms shook as he held himself above me. "You're so perfect for me, Jess. Like a custom-fit glove for me."

His hips pulled out and pistoned forward until I was shaking and on the edge again. "How many times do you want to come?"

"Once. Now. Please." I reached for his hips and pulled, but he resisted.

"Wrong answer." He shifted his hips until he slipped free. "You know I'm all about the details. Let's see how many ways I can make you come." He moved back and dipped his head between my legs again. He massaged the tender flesh gently with his tongue. He probed me firmly with his fingers. First one. Then two. When he added the third, it was a mix of pain and pleasure. Full and ready to burst free, I threaded my fingers through his hair so he couldn't retreat.

He licked and laved and finally pulled the hard nub between his lips and sucked, and I soared. "Mark!" I screamed. He never let up, not even when I begged him to stop. He was determined to leave nothing behind.

Spent with noodle arms and legs, I melted back into the mattress as he climbed between my legs.

CHAPTER TEN

MARK

I had to pull out and focus on her pleasure because those few strokes inside her almost undid me. Loss of control wasn't something I experienced often. I didn't want this to be the one and only time for us, but if it was, I sure as hell didn't want it to be disappointing.

And now that I'd been inside her, tasted her, felt her, I wanted her everywhere there was a surface I could lean her against or place her on. I could see her pinned against the wall of glass in my office. Spread out on the kitchen island of my home. Pressed to the leather seat of my Mercedes.

"If this goes fast, I'm sorry, but it's so damn good, and it's been so long." I pressed into her moist heat and sighed. I could live inside of her forever. Damn all the deals in the world. I could stay in a seedy motel with Jess for the rest of my life.

Slow deliberate strokes brought out that moan I already loved to hear from her. Deep penetrating thrusts pulled her sated body back to life. As the pace quickened, so did her breaths.

"Are you close?"

She clawed at my back, and I continued to pound into her until her body stiffened, her breath halted, and a groan of pure satisfaction slipped from her lips. Her walls tightened and pulsed around me. I pressed forward until I was fully seated inside. I came in hot pulsing waves, the feeling so intense that I was certain my balls had pulled up inside my body. When the last shudder raced through me, I collapsed beside her and pulled her into my arms.

"Feel good?" she whispered in a sleepy voice.

"Good doesn't even begin to describe what that was." She was a perfect fit next to my body, just like she'd been underneath it. Her softness fit into all my hard edges. My chin rested above her head. The smell of her was an aphrodisiac, and I was already on my way to hard again. I was a thirty-two-year-old man, but with Jess, I felt like a sixteen-year-old. "Jess, that was the best sex I've ever had."

When she didn't respond, I knew she had fallen asleep. Her chest rose and fell in a steady beat.

I would have normally fallen asleep myself, but I couldn't take my eyes off her. How had I gotten so lucky? Or was the question more like, how could I be so stupid? Stupid to not see we had both been dancing around the fact we were attracted to one another; stupid to hire her when I should have dated her. Where would tonight take us, and what would happen when we returned to sea level?

Not wanting to think about it, I tucked my body around hers and fell asleep.

The next morning, I woke to the smell of coffee and the hiss of an iron. Jess was standing at the end of the bed dressed in nothing but the *I Put Out for Santa* T-shirt, the hem skimming her milky white thighs. The damn woman was ironing my shirt.

I looked at the clock. It was just after six. "Come back to bed." I patted the empty space beside me. "You're not paid to iron my clothes."

She pressed the steam button, and a cloud of white rose from the material. "I'm not paid to sleep with you either, but I did it because I wanted to."

I lifted up on my elbows, and the sheet dropped to my waist.

Her eyes went to my morning wood standing proud and tall tenting the cover.

"And you'd rather iron my shirt than have sex with me? Was I that bad?" It was a joke—I knew it couldn't have been that bad. I'd made her come twice. I didn't have a pencil dick, and, true to my T-shirt, I had laid a decent amount of pipe before I spilled inside her.

She hung up my shirt and turned off the iron, then crawled across the bed to straddle me. Rotating her hips against my needy erection, she drove me crazy with desire.

"Bad, you ask?" She laughed a sweet little laugh. "It was the best sex I've ever had in my life."

My chest expanded. "The best?"

"I've never had better." She reached over to the nightstand and picked up a cup of coffee. "It's not what you like. This one isn't all thick and sludgy, but it's coffee." She nodded toward the machine on the dresser. One of those single-cup plastic jobs that spit out water with a hint of coffee flavor. "I had little to work with."

I lifted up and took a sip before putting it back on the night-stand. "I want you, Jess." My hands slid under her shirt and tweaked her nipples. She closed her eyes and hummed.

"We really should go."

"I think we owe ourselves one more round."

"Kind of self-indulgent, don't you think?"

I pulled the shirt over her head and cupped her full breasts. Dusky pink nipples pebbled at my touch. She filled my palms perfectly. How was it possible that she was perfect in every way?

"I'm a selfish bastard. I want it all. Can I have it all?"

She stared at me for a long minute, then scooted down to kneel between my spread legs. She unwrapped the sheet from my body like she was unwrapping a long-anticipated gift.

"My turn to get what I want." She didn't hesitate. She opened her lush lips and stuck out her tongue to swipe at the drop glistening at the end of my rod. I was totally screwed; I'd never want to live without her. And when she slid my length into her mouth, I knew I'd never be able to.

"Oh. God. Jess. Jesus, that's so damn good."

She looked up at me with those green eyes that had a way of wrapping around my heart. Her lips tightened around my girth, and she quickened her pace, increased her depth until she nearly swallowed me. I was about three strokes from coming in her mouth when she stopped.

78

"Holy hell." The sheet was fisted in my hands, my jaw so tense that my teeth hurt. "You're killing me."

She rocked her body back and forth, moving up my legs until her sex hovered over my eager length. She lined it up and sank onto my length. Oh, the look on her face—it was enough to make me come, but it was the grinding of her hips that took me to the edge far too fast.

I gripped her hips to stop her. "I don't want you to think I'm a three-strokes-and-out kind of man. I have staying power, but good lord, you have some kind of magic between your legs."

"I'm magic?" She pulled my hands from her hips and held them above my head. Her breasts swayed in front of my mouth like an offering. How could I refuse? I pulled a taut nipple between my teeth and bit lightly. She moaned and pressed down until there wasn't enough room for sweat between us. Her hips rotated and swiveled until my insides coiled up to spring free.

I could have pulled away, but there is something sexy about letting her have control. I was at her mercy, which (if I was honest) was a place I'd been since she started working for me. I liked how that made me feel. Like somehow with Jess, I could be vulnerable and not be less than who I was. It wasn't something I allowed myself with anyone else, but I knew Jess would never abuse the power she held over me.

"Jess," I groaned. "I'm going to come."

"Then come, love. It's what I want." She lifted off of me and pounded back down a half-dozen times. I thrashed against the pillow as the orgasm exploded from my body, and I filled her full of me. She collapsed on top of me. Her breath tickled my chest.

"You're in trouble," I told her with a lack of conviction.

She pulled herself up. The motion sent a shudder from the tip of my length to my toes. "It wasn't good?" She looked down at me, a veil of hair covering her face.

"Oh, baby, it was more than good, but I'm an equal opportunity…man." I almost said *employer*, which would have taken this someplace very different than I wanted to go. "Your turn."

I flipped her over, and she buried my face between her legs. I already knew how to get her aching and wanting with a simple suck, but this morning I wanted her begging for release.

I took her to the edge and brought her down so many times even I was dizzy. When she whimpered and begged, I conceded. I pulled her tight bundle of nerves into my mouth and sucked with a pulsing action that matched her release. My fingers and mouth dripped with her sweet juices as I literally pulled the orgasm from her body. My name on her lips was my reward.

With the back of my hand, I wiped her essence from my face and crawled up her body to kiss her. We lay there in each other's embrace for minutes before she pulled away and spoke.

"Are you ready for reality?"

With my head resting on her shoulder, I played with a lock of her hair. "This seems real."

"It's real at the moment." She turned her body to face me, and my head fell to the pillow. "This is fantasy, and it's an amazing one, but it's not our reality. We didn't come up here for amazing sex."

I bit her shoulder, and she flinched. "We do have amazing sex."

"The best."

I shifted so we were face to face. "Tell me your reality." Deep inside I wanted her to tell me she loved me. It was a stupid thought because outside of work, Jess didn't know me, but I wanted her love, and as soon as I settled all this business stuff, she'd be my next acquisition.

"The pass is still closed. There was an avalanche, and the lanes are covered for a mile."

"Shit. Are you sure?" I tossed off the covers and paced the room naked.

"I checked when I got up."

"Damnit. This deal is the most important thing to me right now." I turned in time to see her pull her frown into a mask of indifference. I was familiar with that mask. I'd worn it all my life. *Never let him see that you're hurt* was my motto growing up. "I'm sorry, Jess. I didn't mean to insinuate that what we did here wasn't important."

"What? I didn't say anything."

She didn't have to; her response was evidence in the silence between us.

"Now what?" I looked around the room. It would never be what it was last night. I'd ruined that with my words. "Shall we head back to Denver?"

"No." She rolled out of bed and went straight to the bathroom. A few minutes later, she appeared already dressed in yesterday's black slacks. "Go take a shower. I have an idea, but I have to make a few calls."

"You think you can salvage this trip?" I wanted to cut my tongue out. I really needed to choose my words more wisely. "What I mean is …"

"Go. Let me do what I do best."

She picked up her phone and turned her back to me. Several seconds later, I heard her say, "Hi, Dad."

CHAPTER ELEVEN

JESS

I t was like Dad was sitting next to the phone because he answered on the first ring. "Did you make it safely to Aspen, honey?"

I let out a groan, not the kind I had last night when Mark coaxed unbelievable pleasure from my body, but the kind that came from frustration mixed with hurt and shit luck.

"The pass is closed."

"What's the plan?"

Dad knew me well. I wasn't the type to roll over and quit—unless, of course, I was dealing with Bethany. I'd learned early on that some fights weren't worth fighting. With Bethany, you might win once, but you'd ultimately lose in the end.

"I was thinking—"

"That's no surprise. You were always the thinker."

I walked to the window and pushed the corner of the curtain open. There was no sun. Large snowflakes floated from a darkened sky to blanket anything that wasn't moving.

"This meeting is really important to Mark." I'd always called him Mr. Cantwell to my parents, and it felt odd to refer to him so informally, but after what we'd done last night, calling him Mr. Cantwell didn't feel right either. "Anyway, I thought if we could make it to your house today, maybe we could borrow the Jeep for the rest of the trip."

There was a long pause. "The only way to make it here is the back roads, Jess. Do you think that's wise?"

"Oh, Dad, I'm way past being wise right now." I let the curtain fall back into place. The bathroom door opened, and Mark walked out in nothing but a towel. "What do you …"

Mark stalked toward me like he was a panther and I was prey.

"Honey, are you there?"

Mark leaned in and kissed my forehead.

"Honey?" Dad's voice echoed on the other end of the line.

"Sorry, Dad. I got distracted." I handed Mark his ironed shirt and pants and turned him back toward the bathroom. "So can we borrow your SUV?"

"Of course you can, but the back roads can be treacherous. Maybe you should wait out the storm." Dad's muffled voice meant he'd put his hand over the receiver. "Mom agrees. You should wait out the storm."

"You don't want me home?"

"Of course we do, but we want you home safe and sound." I heard him relaying my question to Mom, and in my head, I could see her roll her eyes.

"I've got to go, Dad. I'll see you in a few hours." Mark walked out of the bathroom dressed for the boardroom. The only difference about him from every other day was the scruff of a day without shaving, and I had to say it looked damn sexy on him.

"Pack up, we're rerouting through the backcountry."

"Is that wise?"

"Probably not, but it's really the only choice if we want to complete our mission." I folded my T-shirt and shorts and shoved them into my bag. "We are heading through the back roads to my parents' house and borrowing their Jeep."

"So I'm going to meet your parents?" He gave me a smirk. "Should I be worried?"

"Nope, they think you slept on the couch, remember?" When I picked Mark's sweatpants off the floor, he pulled them from my hands.

"Leave them." He plucked at the corner of the shirt peeking from my purse.

"I'm keeping mine. You bought it for me." I shoved it deeper into my bag and zipped it shut.

"I'll buy you something nicer." He grabbed the keys and pocketed them.

"These will always be special to me. I'm keeping them to remind me that something amazing can come from a complete disaster."

Mark pulled me into his arms and kissed me long and hard. It felt like a just-getting-started kiss. But even if he wasn't aware, it was a goodbye kiss. I knew that the minute we walked out of this room, he would become Mr. Cantwell, and I would return to my role as his assistant.

Sorrow gripped my heart because I knew it would be a painful loss. How was I supposed to forget those moments of passion? The magic of his tongue? The touch of his hands? The feel of him inside me? I never would, but we'd said what happened at high altitude would stay at high altitude. And Los Angeles was sea level.

We checked out of the motel and hit the truck stop where I gathered real coffee and food while Mark touched base with the client.

His scowl said everything. "Braxton's plane leaves at noon on Christmas Day. If I'm not there, he's selling to the next in line."

I placed the coffee, donuts, and breakfast sandwiches on the counter. "He sounds like a real Ebenezer."

He pulled a bill from his wallet and paid. "I can't blame him, I'd do the same thing."

"He's a Scrooge, I tell you." I shouldered him in jest, but he didn't budge. Not surprising for a man who appeared carved from granite.

"You wouldn't put someone's life in peril to simply seal a deal," I said, shaking my head. But my voice wasn't as firm as I had intended because that was exactly what he *was* doing ... or was it? In hindsight, it was me pressing his agenda because I didn't want to fail him. "I don't know what's crazier, the fact that he demands the impossible, or the fact that we're willing to give him it." I picked up the bag and walked out of the store.

Mark got in the driver's side. "Do you want to turn back?" There was no irritation in his voice. I was almost convinced that if I said yes, he'd turn around, but then he'd always regret that decision. I didn't need to feel guilty for taking away something that he saw as his. This was his opportunity to right a wrong—to regain a piece of his heritage—to rightfully claim what belonged to him. I wouldn't be another person who took something from him.

Despite the trip being a series of unfortunate events, there were endless moments I'd do all over again. Several hours of pure bliss were a perfect healing balm to the disaster. No, I wasn't ready to throw in the towel just yet. I dug deep to find my smile and can-do spirit.

"If we give up now, everything will have been for nothing." I pulled the visor down and touched the tender purple mark on my forehead. "Let's go, Mr. Cantwell, the most important thing in your life is waiting."

He looked at me with something akin to admiration. "Where to, navigator?"

I guided him through the back roads for the next three hours. The roads were treacherous, but we plugged along at a safe pace.

On the way, he stopped in a town that could be missed with the blink of an eye. A little mom-and-pop country store that sold alpaca wool and fudge. An odd combination.

He kept the car running and told me he'd be out in a second.

Fifteen minutes later, he returned with a bag.

"What's in the bag?"

He pulled out some nicely wrapped packages. "You sacrificed the gifts for your family so I could stay warm. I replaced them."

In his hand was the softest cream-colored beanie that he pulled onto my head. "If we get stuck again, I don't want you cold either."

"You didn't have to buy me anything. I've got a hood." I tapped the triangle of fabric bunched up at my back.

He cupped my face in a way that made me feel cherished. "It hides your beautiful eyes."

The heat of a blush rose to warm my cheeks. "You didn't have to replace the gifts."

He laughed. "I can't have you showing up to your parents' house with nothing. Bad enough they'll think I'm an awful, demanding boss, but if you show up empty-handed, they'll think I don't pay you enough. A fact that is probably true considering all you do for me."

"Thank you for being so considerate." I traced the soft alpaca wool with the tips of my fingers. It was far nicer than anything I could have made.

He turned in his seat. "Jess, it was the least I could do." He started the car and pulled back onto the two-lane highway. "I looked for a gift for your sister, but they didn't have a muzzle or a tranquilizer gun." His shoulders shook in an attempt to contain his laughter.

"That's an awful thing to say." I opened the bag and rummaged through the donuts to find the chocolate-dipped minis.

"Am I misrepresenting her?"

"No, you pegged her spot on." I let out a sigh. "A muzzle would have been perfect."

He reached over and plucked a donut from the package.

"I love the way you share, Jess."

"And what will you share with me?"

"When we get to Aspen, I'll share it all, Jess. We'll sign the contract. Visit the hotel gift shop for new clothes. Have a nice dinner and …"

"And?" Would he want another night?

"And if I can convince you to spend the night, I'd like to share something else."

A quick glance his way told me exactly what he wanted to share with me. Every single hard inch of him pushed against his trousers.

"Look at you." I reached across the seat and rubbed his heavy, hard outline. We were still at high altitude, and he was pressing for another night, so it seemed appropriate. "You've become such a sharer."

He took his foot off the gas. "As much as I love your hands on me. I want to stay alive." He pointed to the outside where snowflakes as big as quarters took a slow dive to the ground. "Keep that thought for later."

"You want a later?"

"Of course I want a later. Last night was amazing, but it wasn't enough." He took my hand and pulled it to his lips.

Caught up in his words and his touch, I almost missed the turn into my parents' driveway.

"Right. Right. Right."

"Damn straight. I love the enthusiasm."

"No, I mean turn right." He swung the car into the barely paved drive, nearly hitting the big pine tree at the end. The tires spun as we made our way to the cabin at the top of the hill.

Bouncing on the balls of her feet was Mom. Behind her was Dad, tugging on his coat.

"Honey, you made it." Dad trotted down the steps to the car. He whistled when he got a good look at the damage.

"Dad, stay there. We'll be right up."

"I'll help you with your things."

I looked back at the beaten-up car. "We don't have anything to bring in. Besides, we're staying just long enough to trade this beauty for yours."

Mom and Dad looked at each other before Dad broke the silence. "You aren't going anywhere."

CHAPTER TWELVE

MARK

Jim Stone led us into the rustic log cabin. The air smelled like cinnamon and spice. A fire crackled in the stone fireplace, and a space was carved out in the corner for the Christmas tree the Stones would cut down and decorate on Christmas Eve.

The house was warm and cozy. A far cry from the glass and steel of my penthouse. Plaid throws were draped over the arms of the worn leather sofa, begging for a body to cover.

All the way up here, Jess had talked about her family and the holidays. How they trekked out into the forest on Christmas Eve day and picked out the perfect tree. How her father used Grandpa's ax to cut it down. Once it was up, they would sing Christmas carols and eat cookies while they covered the tree with decorations made over the years.

Spending time with loved ones was a foreign concept to me. If I was lucky, I got to sleep in and order room service before Dad was in motion.

"Scotch?" Jim held up a bottle of Macallan. "Looks like you could use a drink."

"Yes, sir, that would be great." I looked past him to the kitchen where Jess and her mom were locked in a hug.

"Finally," a voice came from the stairs. "It seems like we're always waiting for you." The owner of the voice stepped off the stairs and took in her surroundings like a detective at a fresh crime scene. "And who is this?"

"You must be Bethany." I set the tumbler down on the wooden coffee table and offered my hand. She laid hers in mine like she was royalty and left it there as if waiting for me to kiss her ring.

"I am, and you must be Mr. Cantwell."

"Call me Mark." I shook her hand, pulled mine back, and looked toward Jess who had an I-told-you-so look on her face.

I turned away from Bethany and focused on Jim. "What's this about not going anywhere?"

"All the main passes are closed. You arrived in the middle of an Albuquerque low."

I picked up the tumbler and took a drink, letting the alcohol create a slow burn down to my stomach. "Excuse my ignorance, but I have no idea what that means."

Bethany walked between her father and me. She picked up the scotch and poured herself a tumbler, then ruined the quality liquor by adding several cubes of ice.

"What Daddy's saying is that the storm came in from New Mexico, which means it's twice as wet and twice as much."

Jess approached with two decorated cookies: one a snowman and one a Santa. "These are the best. Pick one."

I saw the sparkle in her eye, but I was sure no one else did. This was a private joke between the two of us. I reached for the snowman. "I hear you have a thing for Santa. I'll leave that one for you."

She stuck her tongue out and licked the frosting off the top, arousing insane jealousy of a cookie … among other things. I'd been the recipient of her tongue, and the experience was nothing short of amazing.

With an expression designed for poker, she looked at her father. "So I met this guy whose middle name was Santa. Can you believe that?"

"Was he hot?" her sister asked.

"Amazingly so."

"You should date him. Isn't it time you found a man?" Bethany walked to Jess and rubbed at the dark circles under Jess's eyes. Circles I'd put there by keeping her up late. "You're not getting any younger, you know."

Jess swiped her sister's hand away. "I'm doing all right."

Jim walked to the kitchen. I wasn't sure whether it was a survival instinct or a real craving for a cookie. I should have followed him, but I didn't want to leave Jess alone with her sister, unprotected.

"You spend all your time at work." She looked me up and down. "I mean, your boss is handsome, but really, Jess. He's not going to keep your bed warm and put a child in your belly."

"Geez, Bethany. Mark is my boss. Can you spare him the drama for a day?"

She looked at Mark. "Jess might be a rock star at work, but here she's an opening act." She tipped back the glass and drained it.

"Do you really have to go for the jugular every minute of the day? How awful does your life have to be that you take down others to lift yourself up?"

Before Bethany could attack again, Jess's mom Amy approached the group. "Dad says he'll keep checking in case any of the passes open. The storm is supposed to get worse overnight, then clear on Christmas Day." She looked toward me with Jess's green eyes. "I'm sorry, Mr. Cantwell, but it looks like you're stuck with us."

Bethany sat on the couch with a heavy thud.

"Where's Matt?" Jess asked her sister.

"He's not coming. He's on call this weekend." She poured herself another three fingers of scotch.

"Where's Ben?" Jess picked another Santa off the plate her mother had set on the table. "I just love Santa."

I gave Jess my best Santa-wants-you-again look without letting her family in on to what Jess and I had shared the night before. By her smile, I knew she got every silent word I sent.

Bethany took a sip and looked toward the stairs. "It's nap time." She watched Jess nibble the black boots off the cookie. "Do you really think you need another cookie?"

Jess grabbed two more and dramatically bit the heads off both. "Definitely."

"Sweetie," her mom said, "since the roads are closed, I've prepared the guest room for Mr. Cantwell."

"Please call me Mark," I asked. "I do appreciate your hospitality. It's been quite a trip, and honestly very little has gone right."

"Tell me about the trip."

"Jess told you the story." I sipped my scotch and watched Jess. Each time I looked at her, something inside me did a flip, making my heart race and my dick twitch. "canceled flight, a reroute, a car accident." I brushed Jess's bangs aside to show the bruise on her head.

"Oh my God, I thought it was a fender bender. Are you okay?" Jess's mom went straight into caretaker mode—something I wasn't accustomed to experiencing. I did have a nanny like that once, but my father accused her of making me too soft and fired her. So my next nanny came straight out of central casting for villains. Even her name sounded mean: Ms. Killkyd. She was the devil in white loafers.

"Yes, I'm fine." Jess gave her mom a hug. "My head is the least of our problems." She looked at me to finish the story.

"I'm afraid she's right. We left the car locked but came back to find the windows punched out and our bags gone."

Bethany bolted up straight. "Someone stole my present?"

"No. Yours was in my purse."

"Thank God." Bethany fell back into the sofa.

"Bethany, sometimes you're too much." Jess's mom stood and shook her head, then turned in our direction. "Show Mark his room. I'll see if I can scrounge up some clothes for you both."

"Ready for the tour?" Jess walked toward the stairs, and I followed right behind. There was no way I was staying in the same room as her sister. I'd rather be flayed and doused in rubbing alcohol.

At the top of the stairs, Jess pointed to the two rooms at the end of hallway and said the one on the right was Bethany's, and the one on the left was her parent's. She turned into the first room and said, "This is your room." Jess walked into the room decorated in plaid and pine cones. She pointed to a door to the left. "That's the bathroom. My room is on the other side."

As soon as we cleared the door, I shut it. Two steps and she was in my arms. My mouth covered her lips. My hands covered her ass, and for the first time in hours, I felt like my world wasn't crashing around me. I whispered against her soft full lips, "You're the only thing that makes sense today."

She cupped my face. "It's been a total shit storm, hasn't it?"

"Storm … yes. Shit … no." Her mouth opened to reply, and my tongue slipped inside. She tasted like icing and sexiness. My lips pressed so tightly against hers that our teeth touched. "I want you so bad, Jess. Last night wasn't enough. This morning wasn't enough. It will never be enough."

She leaned into me until her chest pressed against mine. I could feel her heartbeat race to catch mine, or was that mine racing to catch hers?

Her hands pressed against my chest to push me away, but her fingers gripped my shirt so I couldn't go too far. "We can't. Not here. Not now. My parents …"

She was right. It was disrespectful to her parents who offered me shelter from the storm. "When the snow clears, come to

Aspen with me. I need you." I wanted her under me and over me, but I wanted something more. I wanted inside her heart as well as her body, and that was new to me.

She laid her head on my chest, and we both took deep breaths. "I won't leave my family on Christmas."

I had no right to expect her to choose me. Her devotion to family was in line with all the qualities that I admired about her.

For nearly a year, I'd gotten to know Jess the assistant, but the past two days, I had gotten to know Jess the woman, and she was everything I wasn't. She was patient, and measured, and wise beyond her years. She was forgiving and graceful. She was the half I was missing, and once I closed this deal, I intended to prove to her that I could be more than her boss.

If I were honest with myself, Jess could rule my entire world if I allowed it, but could I let myself be that vulnerable? Trust hadn't been a word in my vocabulary since my own father stole what was mine.

The door vibrated with a knock, and Jess jumped back and disappeared into the connecting bathroom. I adjusted the bulge in my pants and answered.

Jess's mom looked behind me as if she expected her daughter to be in my room. In her arms was a pile of clothes ranging from pants to sweaters to boots. "Give these a try. Jim is a bit more healthy around the middle, but you're roughly the same height." She looked down at the boots that were nearly new. "He didn't like these. Said they were too modern. If you can fit in an eleven, they're yours."

"Thank you, ma'am, an eleven is perfect." It was, and *modern* wasn't what I'd call the Doc Martens. *Timeless* was more like it.

"Call me Amy. It looks like we're adopting you for a day or two. Go ahead and relax for a bit. We're having roasted chicken for dinner in about an hour." She turned around and walked out. I peeked out the door and watched her pick up another stack of clothes and go two doors down to where I assumed Jess was staying.

When I heard voices, I walked into the bathroom to make sure Jess wasn't still hiding in there.

"Your sister generously offered a few of her things. I added a few of my own," her mother said.

I shouldn't have been eavesdropping, but the minute *generous* and *Bethany* came out in the same sentence, I was hooked. It was like watching a soap opera unfold one scene at a time.

"Come on, Mom, what did you have to threaten her with to give up a pair of her jeans?" The sound of rustling fabric floated under the closed bathroom door.

"Nothing. I swear." There was a moment of complete silence, and I was about to turn around and walk into my room, until Amy finally continued, "Okay, I told her she could open the first Christmas present if she showed some Christmas spirit."

I could almost see Jess roll her eyes.

"Mom, are you sure she wasn't switched at birth? I mean she isn't like the rest of us."

"Oh, honey, Bethany has her own charm."

I leaned against the door and heard Jess growl. It wasn't the same gravelly sound she made just before she came, but rather the sound of frustration mixed with disbelief.

"I'd like to be a recipient of some of that charm."

Her mom dismissed the last sentence. "Come downstairs and help me with dinner. I want to know more about that handsome boss of yours."

CHAPTER THIRTEEN

JESS

When Mom left the room, I sank onto my bed next to the borrowed clothes. I pulled the jeans Bethany donated from the pile.

"Generous, my ass," I said out loud. The jeans she donated were ones she'd left behind when she went off to college. Clothes she'd discarded at least eight years ago, but that my mom couldn't seem to let go.

The bathroom door creaked open, and Mark slipped into my room. He looked odd standing amongst my track trophies and Leonardo DiCaprio posters. Another blast from the past that my mother couldn't relinquish. We'd always be her little girls, and she was safeguarding all the keepsakes to prove it.

"Your ass is perfect and will look amazing in anything you wear." He took the jeans and held them up. "Very retro."

I swiped them from his grip. "That's a nice word for *old*."

"Where were we?" He leaned in and brushed his lips across mine. He fell to his knees in front of me and threaded his fingers through the back of my hair. "I think we were here." His scent enveloped me like a hug.

Every year I came home to the same thing; every year I left with the pledge that the next year would be different, and yet it was always the same. This year it wasn't. I had Mark, and although I didn't have him as my significant other, he lent me his strength with his words and his touch and his kisses.

"We weren't really here." I palmed the scruff of his face, letting my fingers brush the two-day-growth of his beard. "We were in your room, and I was telling you how much I wanted you, but I couldn't have you."

He pressed me back onto my bed and covered me with his body. "I don't remember hearing how much you want me. Can you tell me again?"

"Oh, Mr. Cantwell, your ego needs no boosting. Besides, my parents think you're my boss."

He ground his hardness against me, and I groaned. "I am your boss, and you're probably right. But I love every word that comes from your lips except *no*." He looked at me with longing. "Staying away from you will be hard."

I snaked my hand between our bodies and rubbed my palm up and down his length. "Staying with me appears to create a harder situation."

He lifted from my body. "Now you're being cruel." He dipped in and bit my lower lip, letting it pop from between his lips. "As much as it pains me, I'll respect your wishes." He looked over his shoulder toward the bathroom and his room. "You know where I am if you change your mind."

He pushed off the bed and left me lying there wanting and wishing for something more. I closed my eyes to remember the moment he entered me for the first time. It was magical. He'd already drawn out the tension in my body. All there had been left to do was enjoy, and I'd done just that—every thrusting inch of him. How the hell was I supposed to get through two nights without him much less a lifetime?

I pulled the snow globe from my purse and set it on my nightstand. I had it and the sweet ache between my thighs to remind me of the best night of my life.

"Jess, come down and help me," Mom's voice rose from downstairs.

"Coming," I said. I passed Mark's door and felt a twinge of regret that we couldn't have more.

Mom was in the kitchen with her hand up a chicken's patooty. Another victim sat next to the first waiting for her assault. "Grab the salt and pepper, honey."

I sprinkled the birds liberally with salt and pepper while Mom shoved citrus fruit and rosemary into the empty cavities.

"Tell me why this boss of yours has you working over the holidays." She arranged the birds in a roasting pan and placed them into the heated oven.

Without being asked, I started cleaning the green beans by snipping off the ends and breaking them into bite-sized pieces. Mom and I always worked in tandem seamlessly.

"It's a deal that could only happen now. Mark and the seller need the transaction to be complete before New Year for tax reasons."

"There's a whole week between Christmas and New Year. The poor man is chasing after a deal and will miss the holidays with his family."

I gathered the green beans and put them in a frying pan. They would be wonderful when cooked with garlic and butter.

"He doesn't have family. He doesn't celebrate Christmas." As I said that out loud, I felt a deep sense of sadness for Mark. All these years he'd been missing out.

"Well, we'll be his adopted family, and he'll celebrate with us in this house." Mom looked down at the jeans Bethany gave me and shook her head.

They made perfect clam diggers. More suited for a walk on the beach than a trek in the snow but they would do. At least they hugged my ass.

Dad came in from the back deck. He ruffled the flakes out of his hair and blew a *brr* sound from his lips. "Where's that boss of yours?"

"Right here, sir." Trudging down the stairs was none other than Mark, but he wasn't the man who showed up in custom suits and designer ties. This guy was straight out of a paper towel commercial. Dad's old blue jeans hung low on his hips. The red plaid flannel hung open to reveal a black T-shirt stretched tight across his chest. On his feet were a pair of Doc Martens. The man was a chameleon.

"I thought while the girls prepared dinner, you and I could chop some wood. It's going to be a cold one tonight." Dad handed Mark a pair of work gloves and a knit cap.

There was no stopping the laughter that burst from my lips. Everyone looked at me like I'd lost my mind, but the thought of Mark chopping wood didn't compute.

"What?" Mark pulled the cap on his head.

"Nothing. I just …"

"You just what, Jess?" Dad asked as he shoved a spare coat into Mark's hands.

"Nothing." The suppressed laughter shook my shoulders. "Mark's not really the outdoor type. He's more Armani than ax."

"He's a man, and ax swinging will come as naturally to a man as …" All eyes went to Dad as his sentence trailed off into silence.

"As what, Dad?" I lifted my brow, waiting for him to complete the sentence more suited for a man cave than the family kitchen.

"Bossing and breeding," Bethany said, walking in with Ben's hand in hers.

Relief washed over Dad when he saw his grandson. "Hey, buddy. Ask your mom to put you in a coat. Mark and I will teach you how to do man stuff." Ben was probably the best thing Bethany ever gave them. He was definitely the best thing she'd ever given me.

"Aunt Jess!" The little imp raced toward me and flung himself into my arms.

I tousled his hair. "Hey, squirt, you want to do man things?" He wiggled down my body and raced for his boots and coat.

"I am a man." He fisted his hands to his sides and puffed out his chest. The only things he was missing were a cape and a breastplate with a big *S*.

I nodded my head. "I know, and since Mr. Cantwell is new to this caveman behavior, maybe you can teach him a thing or two."

When I looked up, Mark gave me an expression that screamed, *you're in big trouble*.

Too bad that trip to Aspen together wasn't going to happen because I would've loved to see where that look could lead.

"You want to chop the salad or make the dressing?" I didn't give Bethany an option to say no. "I realize you have people to do everything normally, but surely you can help prepare dinner here."

She reached for the bowl of freshly washed lettuce and tore the leaves into bite-sized pieces while I mixed the salad dressing.

"Your boss seems nice enough." She stared out the window where Mark and Ben stood watching Dad give a safety lesson. "Mom says you two had to sleep together last night."

"Oh Bethany, that is not what I said." Mom sliced a loaf of French bread in half and slathered it with butter and garlic. "I said they were stranded together."

"Same thing," Bethany said with a shrug.

"How did Matt get stuck with Christmas rounds this year? He has seniority, right? Surely, he could have delegated to someone else."

Bethany swallowed hard. She wiped her hands on a towel and reached for Dad's bottle of scotch. Generally, she wasn't much of a hard liquor drinker. She preferred drinks that were pink and came with umbrellas, so the action told me what her mouth refused to say: There was trouble in paradise.

"My husband, unlike your boss, is considerate and took the shift so others could spend the holiday with their families."

I snatched the tumbler from her hand and stole a drink. "I'm here, aren't I?" I wanted to defend Mark, but I couldn't, without betraying his confidences. He didn't understand what Christmas meant because he'd never experienced it.

"Yes, you are," Mom said with more exuberance than warranted. "I love it when you all come home." Mom glanced out the window at Dad. "It's a good thing Mark is here. At least Dad will have someone else to bond with."

While Bethany made the salad and Mom peeled the potatoes. I leaned against the back door and watched as Mark swung the ax. His brute strength severed the log in one swing. As if he felt me watching, he looked up at me and smiled as if to say, *take that.*

Watching the three of them together was heartwarming. They both took turns helping Ben chop the wood. My sister's son seemed to grow taller under their words of encouragement. I thought back to Mark commenting on his nannies and wondered whether Ben was better off because he had one. Like Mark's father, my sister wasn't the warmest person, so I hoped the little guy had someone who filled in the holes.

They loaded up their arms and carried the wood inside.

"Hey, Jess, your dad says you make the best hot chocolate. What are the chances we can bribe you to make us some?" Mark said teasingly while Ben put on that sad little face I couldn't resist, the one that pleaded with his father's baby blue eyes.

"Hot chocolate coming up." I walked to Mark and plucked the knit cap off his head. His hair stuck out in every direction, just like it had this morning when I'd finished riding him. "You want a dose of adult in yours?"

He looked at my sister and nodded. He caught on fast. The only way to survive in her presence was to drink yourself numb.

CHAPTER FOURTEEN

MARK

She was simply stunning. It didn't matter that the snowman sweater with the plastic moving eyes was ridiculous. Nor did it matter that the jeans her sister gave her were from an era gone by. Jess wore them with confidence and grace, and she was beautiful.

I could have stood there and watched her all day, but Jim insisted we watch football. I sensed he was on a mission to test my manliness.

I helped Ben out of his jacket and lifted him to my shoulders. He squealed with delight. It was so easy to please a kid. A knot formed in my stomach when I thought about my father and how little effort he put into me. Never once had I taken a ride on his shoulders.

I looked up into Ben's eyes so full of wonder. "Your grandfather wants to watch football. How about it, champ?"

He wiggled around, and I held tight. "Can we have cookies?"

I looked toward the women who were all shaking their heads. "Nope. Too close to dinner."

He hung his head. "Dang it."

"After dinner?" I looked back at the women who now nodded their heads in agreement. I was catching on fast. My respect for Jim grew.

Jim fell into his throne, a leather recliner set at a perfect angle to the big-screen television, and turned on the Broncos-Jets game. I flopped into the corner of the couch where Ben climbed down from my shoulders and snuggled up to my side. I had no experience with kids, but I liked this one. He seemed to have come out unscathed by his mother's bad attitude thus far.

Ben tugged on my plaid shirt. "Tomorrow we get to cut down the Christmas tree. I'm old enough this year."

"That's exciting."

"We get to decorate it and put presents under the tree. Do you have a present for me?" I glanced back at Bethany, who shrugged her shoulders and made no excuses for her son. It appeared the apple didn't fall far from her tree.

Really, though, it wasn't a surprise that Ben would focus on presents. First of all, he was a kid, but probably more importantly, his mom was all about what she got. I didn't understand how two completely different women could have been raised in the same house.

"Ben, that wasn't a nice question." Jess placed two cups of steaming hot cocoa on the table in front of us before she brought one to her father. "Christmas isn't about the presents. It's about the people." Jess took a seat in the recliner on the other side of the sofa. She was too far away, but at the perfect place where I could stare at her and people would think I was watching the game. She was far more interesting than pigskin and goalposts.

The little critter sat on the edge of his seat and pushed the top of a marshmallow. He laughed when it bobbed down and floated up. Had life ever been that simple for me?

"I know." Ben sighed. "Sasha told me it wasn't the gift that counted but the thought behind the gift." He blew on his cocoa and then turned to me with what I'd call the perfect boardroom look. Serious. Confident. No nonsense. "I don't have a present for you either, but I'm going to draw you a picture because handmade gifts are the best. They contain heart. That's what Sasha says. Can you draw me a picture too?"

"You bet, sport."

When halftime came, Jim turned his focus from the television to me. "So, Mark, where's your family?"

Any talk of my family required copious amounts of alcohol. I pulled my lips to the cup and sipped; this was no hot chocolate, but the best Irish coffee I'd ever had—Jess had added enough "adult" to it to make my nose burn. I gave her a grateful look before saying, "My mother has passed, and my father has passed through my life."

"What about a girlfriend? Surely a successful lad like yourself has a girl." He sipped his hot beverage and tapped a fist to his chest. "That's some good cocoa." He winked at Jess.

This interaction between child and father was fascinating to me. Mine came home long enough to complain to the staff about my upbringing and left again. I got a regular dose of judgment, enough to last a lifetime, never a wink or a smile.

"I've never really had the time to seek a relationship."

"No one? That's a shame. Family is everything. You can have all the money in the world, but if you don't have family, you're still poor. Family is a man's gold."

"Dad, Mark is far from poor. Not everyone is designed for family life."

"Nonsense. A man needs a good woman in his life." He looked over his shoulder toward the kitchen. I knew he was glancing at Amy. They were really a perfect couple, and I saw the love and affection he had for her written plainly on his face.

"There is someone I'm interested in, but it's too soon to tell. I'm pretty sure she'd be my gold, but I fear I'd be the gravel left after a lucky strike."

I stared straight at Jess, hoping she'd understand that it was of her I spoke and seeing her smile, I knew that she knew.

"Just remember, son. Family is everything."

"I'll remember that." It was a foreign concept, but then again, so was eating sushi until I gave it a try.

"Dinner's ready," Amy called from the table. While Jim had been talking about family, Bethany and her mom were setting the table.

Jim took the head of the table while Amy sat on the opposite side. Bethany and Ben sat on one side, leaving Jess and me on the other.

I'd never had a regular family dinner, so I waited to see how it all went down. It started with a prayer of thanks. Silently I said my own prayer of thanks to the snow gods who'd stranded me with Jess. It wasn't what I had planned, but something told me it was what I needed.

As soon as grace had finished, Jim asked, "Could you please pass the potatoes, lovey?" Amy passed the heaping bowl of butter-laden goodness, and Jim scooped a large helping onto his plate. The next thing I knew, bowls and plates were flying around the table. It was as if Jim serving himself was the green light for everyone else to eat.

It was a simple meal, but one of the best tasting I'd had in a long time. That was until Bethany soured it with her negativity.

"Is my sister a good secretary?"

Even though Jess wasn't touching me, I sensed her stiffen. Trying to be discreet, I moved my hand under the table and gave her thigh a gentle rub. She immediately softened at my touch.

"Jess is an executive assistant."

Bethany turned toward her sister and said, "Isn't that the same thing as a secretary?"

"Not at all," I said. "Jess is instrumental in every facet of my business. She does research and proposals and prepares contracts. She's the perfect liaison with clients."

Bethany looked between us. "So she's like a librarian who types." A smug smile marred her face.

It suddenly dawned on me that Bethany didn't feel superior to Jess. She knew she was inferior so she did everything in her power to make my Jess's life miserable. *My Jess.* I liked the sound of that. And because I did, I acted in defense of what I considered mine.

"Tell me, Bethany. What did you study in school? You did go to school, right?"

I looked around the table, and all eyes were on the wicked sister. Amy and Jim had probably spent years trying to bridge the gap between the two girls, but you can't shore up a relationship when one pillar stands on quicksand and the other on solid concrete.

"Of course I did. I studied hospital management."

"And is that where you work? At a hospital?" I knew she didn't work, but she didn't know that I knew.

"No, I don't work."

I gave her my classic *I don't understand* look: squinted eyes mixed with a look of confusion. "If you don't work, what is it you do all day?" I was leading her down a path of no return.

"I raise my son."

"Motherhood is a full-time job, I hear." I looked over at Ben. "He's a great kid. Who's the Sasha he keeps talking about?"

"My nanny," Ben chimed in. "We have her and Rosa, our cook, and Tia, our housekeeper. Michael does the lawn, and Stephen takes care of the pool in the summer."

"You have a lot of help to raise one child."

She fidgeted in her seat. "What can I say, I married well."

"I hear there's an art to that." I smoothed my hand over Jess's thigh and felt my heart lurch when she squeezed my hand in hers. "In fact, I think there's an entire show on marrying well. Something about housewives of Beverly Hills. I hear it's quite the depiction of women who marry well." I shake my head. "Not very flattering, I'm afraid."

"I live in Connecticut," she said with an edge as sharp as a switchblade.

"You should check to see if they're casting there. I'm sure you'd fit right in, being that the only requisite is marrying well." It wasn't really my place to put her in hers, but I was tired of her taking jabs at Jess. I didn't like the way she looked at my girl. I didn't like the way she talked to her.

When I finished talking, everyone was staring at me with a different face. Amy and Jim sat with looks of respect like I'd said something they wished they could have. Ben just looked at me with a blank expression. Bethany looked at me with daggers. When I turned to look at Jess, all I saw was love.

I rose from my seat, with my near empty plate in my hand, to break the silence. "Can I help clean up?"

"No need, Mark. The girls and I can get it," Amy said.

I walked my plate into the kitchen, set it on the counter next to the sink, and returned to the dining room. "Then, if you don't mind, I have to go over a contract."

"Do you need help?" Jess too rose from the table with her empty plate in her hand.

"No. You enjoy your family. I'll be fine." I turned and walked up the stairs to my room.

Just before I closed the door, I heard Bethany say, "He's an a-hole," followed by Jess's comment that I was amazing.

I had no idea what family dinners were supposed to be like, but this one had gotten my adrenaline pumping. Jim and Amy were gracious hosts though weak when it came to putting Bethany in her place. Ben was as cute as could be, and it was a wonder he wasn't already poisoned with his mother's venom. Then there was Jess, who took it all in. Deep inside I knew she knew what I did—her sister felt inferior—and that was why she didn't fight back. She was a bigger person than I would ever be.

A few minutes passed and there was a slight knock on the door. "Come in," I said from my perch on the bed.

In walked Jess with a glass of milk and a plate of cookies. "I didn't want you to miss out on dessert."

CHAPTER FIFTEEN

JESS

I said the words like I was sitting on the plate rather than frosted sugar cookies.

"Close the door and come sit by me." Mark set his computer to the side and patted the space next to him.

I set the offerings down on the table next to the bed and climbed up beside him.

"I don't want to interrupt what you're doing."

"You're not interrupting." He turned his computer screen to face me. He had Googled *Christmas traditions*.

"You really have no idea how to celebrate, do you?"

He shook his head. "I'm not totally inept. I know some carols. What I'm really disappointed in is the fact that nowhere in your parents' house is mistletoe. There are Santas and snowmen everywhere but not a single sprig of mistletoe. Why is that?"

I snuggled in next to him. "It's poisonous, and Mom is afraid Ben will eat it, but we can pretend there's a piece hanging over our heads right now." I turned my face up to his and melted when his lips touched mine.

"If this is dessert, I'll take a second helping." His kisses were like wine—sweet and intoxicating enough to want more, but not enough to became stupid drunk on them. He did other things with his tongue that made me feel dizzy and out of control. "Are you dessert, Jess?"

We slipped down so we lay side by side. His fingers threaded through my hair, pulling me deeper into the kiss. His free hand slipped under my silly sweater and made its way to my breasts.

"My parents think I'm helping you with a project."

"You are." He pulled my sweater from my body and ran his lips across my stomach. "You're helping me get my head straight."

I felt his head. It was indeed straight, not to mention hard and pressed firmly against my thigh.

I glanced at the door and back at Mark. "You're a bad influence. What if someone walks in?"

In one swift movement, he leapt over me and locked the door. On his way back, he discarded his overshirt, his T-shirt, and his shoes.

"No one is walking in now." He unbuttoned the jeans and let them fall to the floor. There he was standing in his full naked glory. His rod pointed directly at me like Uncle Sam's finger in a recruitment poster, only so much bigger. "You make the call, Jess. I'll let you go if that's what you want, but if you stay,

I'll make this the best dessert experience of your life. One word. Yes or no?"

I chewed the inside of my cheek. How was I supposed to turn down a dessert offer like that? One more glance at the locked door, and I unhooked my bra and dragged the jeans down my hips. "You can't make me scream."

His look said he had something different in mind. "Oh, baby, I'm going to make you scream on the inside." He tugged my jeans free and tossed them with the other discarded clothes on the floor. With hunger in his eyes, he slunk up my body until his face was inches away from my core.

He breathed a stream of air across my sex that both heated and chilled me. "I can't believe I'm doing this."

He ran his tongue through my slick heat. "I can't believe you made me wait this long." Long strokes up and down my sex had me lifting my hips into his mouth. I pulled my fist to mine and pushed the pad of my palm against my lips to stifle the sounds coming from me: deep guttural sounds that erupted from my soul; primal noises that I couldn't have stopped if my life had depended on it. Mark licked and sucked with vigor until my thighs shook and my core clenched.

Afraid that my moans would bring unneeded attention, I turned my face and whimpered my release into the soft cotton pillowcase. My body quaked and quivered as he brought me down with long strokes of his velvet tongue.

Base need was what I felt when he crawled up my body and nudged at my entrance. "Hurry." I gripped his hips and pulled.

His head shook back and forth ever so slowly. "I won't be hurrying today, love. A dessert this sweet and rich should be savored and enjoyed, not rushed."

A flex of his hips pushed him inside me. Just enough that I knew he was there, but not enough to satisfy. "I need more."

He kissed me gently and whispered against my lips, "I'll give you everything." In and out he slid his hard length. Never giving me all of him, but never denying me either. He pressed and retreated until he was fully seated and pulsing inside me.

"I'll take it all," I said out of desperation. "When you're inside me, it's the only time I feel complete." I wanted to take those words back, but I couldn't. They were pure and honest. It didn't matter if this was short term or something that would bloom into forever—I still wanted Mark to feel my love for him. I was positive that he'd never felt love without expectations before.

"So damn perfect." He increased the speed and pressure until my body began to vibrate from within. My core heated and coiled into a delicious quivering mass. Braced above me, he looked at me with eyes full of passion. Passion I had ignited in him.

"So good," I panted. My fingernails dug into his butt with each thrust. He shifted and brought the pressure to my tight bundle of nerves, and those uncontrollable sounds surfaced again until Mark covered my moans with his mouth. I pulled up my knees so each thrust hit me just where I needed.

My release started in my toes and snaked up my body until my insides felt like a kaleidoscope of butterflies circling inside of me. The heat peaked and exploded from within. My walls pulsed around him, sucking him deeper inside me until he stilled and the pulse of his release splashed against my insides. He breathed the sound of his pleasure against my lips before he collapsed beside me. His head lay on my chest while his fingers danced across my stomach.

We lay in each other's arms. The room spun around me as I regained my breath and composure. The man made me light-headed on a good day, downright dizzy on a great day. Today was a great day.

"Hey, Jess." My sister's voice came from the other room. I bolted out of bed and dove for my clothes, but I wasn't fast enough. She'd already walked through the bathroom and stood in the doorway, looking at my naked body. Her gaze went to Mark, who was pulling the sheet over his lower half.

"Oh. My. God," she said in a whisper-yell. "You're screwing your boss. That's how you got that job."

Mark leapt from the bed, letting the sheet fall as he rushed to confront my sister.

"I won't have you make something beautiful into something ugly."

She looked down at his length, which was still impressive even as it softened. "You're doing your secretary. How cliché is that?"

Mark and I looked at each other and snapped, "Executive assistant."

Bethany looked at me with an evil glint in her eyes. "I hope you get paid extra for that service."

Mark took another step forward, and Bethany escaped out the door and down the hallway to her room. I tugged on my pants and pulled on the ugly sweater. "I'll take care of it. Get dressed and have a scotch with my dad. This is going to get ugly. No matter what you hear, keep my parents and Ben downstairs."

I kissed him firmly on the lips and stalked down the hallway to my sister's room. I walked inside and slammed the door behind me. Bethany looked for an escape, but there wasn't one.

"What the hell is your problem?" My voice rose to a deafening pitch.

"My problem? I'm not the one sleeping with my boss."

I fisted up my hands and clenched them behind my back, so afraid I'd let one of them loose on her face. "No, you didn't wait to get the job, you screwed him during the interview. Got pregnant and forced the bastard to marry you."

Pain sliced her smug expression. "Why would you say that?"

"Because it's the truth." Last year, during our annual Christmas gathering, Matt had had a little too much to drink. "Your husband told me over a bottle of scotch."

"That's not true. It was love at first sight. We took one look at each other, and that was it."

I paced her room, wondering how much I dared divulge. "Was that the first time he saw you walking into his office, or when you sat in the seat across from him and pulled a Sharon Stone *Basic Instinct* move? Matt said you shaved."

She let out a gasp followed by a flood of tears. "You don't know what it's like being your sister."

I let my fists unfurl. "No, but I do know what it's like being yours, and it isn't much fun."

"You're taller and prettier, and you got Mom's green eyes while I got the shit-brown ones. You graduated summa cum laude, and I barely graduated. You have a skinnier ass and nice set of tits. Your hair, well, what can I say, it's perfect like the rest of you." She buried her face in her hands and wailed.

It was hard to show empathy for someone who'd never shown signs of having an empathy gene herself, but I'd always tried to lead by example, so I sat on her bed and pulled her into my arms.

"You're a good person, Bethany; you really are. It's just that you hide that goodness behind this person you created. She's a bitch."

"I'm not a good person." She rubbed her snotty nose into my shoulder. "Tell me one thing that's good about me."

I didn't want to take too long to come up with something, so I said the obvious. "Ben. He's everything that's good about you."

She sniffled in and breathed out a choppy breath. "He is pretty great."

"He's amazing. He loves you. He looks at you like you're his hero. Be his hero. Play with him. Tell him you love him. Let him paint your nails with Sharpies and draw your picture with crayons. Roast marshmallows with him, and sit in the center of a pile of Legos and build a masterpiece. Give him memories, not things. He'll never not love the gift of your time."

I thought about Mark and felt sad that he'd missed those opportunities with his mother and father, but at least he'd had a wonderful nanny early on who planted ideas about love and loyalty and right and wrong. Mark turned out okay because he'd had one person in his life who had made a difference. I wanted that for Ben—but I wanted that person to be his mom, not hired help.

"What about your boss? Do you think it's wise that you're sleeping with him?"

"No, probably not, but it's wonderful while it lasts. He's a good man."

"How long have you been in a relationship?"

I flopped back on her bed and covered my eyes with my arm. "Since yesterday."

"Oh. My. God."

I rolled over and pulled her down so she was forced to look at me. "It wasn't planned, but neither was the snowstorm, the crash, or the motel. It kind of just happened."

"What happens now?"

"I don't know. Don't take this wrong … I won't force him into anything. What happens is what happens. We're both grown-ups. We'll deal with the fallout when and if it comes."

"You love him, don't you?" She pushed my hair from my face. We hadn't lain in bed and shared our secrets since junior high. I'd missed the girl she was back then.

I hated to tell my sister the truth because in a bad moment she'd use it against me, but this moment called for honesty because saying I didn't love him felt like a betrayal to Mark.

"I do. I've been in love with him since the beginning."

"I can see it in your eyes. Kind of pisses me off."

I laughed. "Because you don't feel that way about Matt?"

She swiped at the tears rolling down her face. "No. Because I do, and I don't think he feels the same about me."

I sat up and pulled her up with me. "That's not true. He does love you, and he loves Ben. He just doesn't know how to please you."

Bethany sat in silence for a minute. "He doesn't want to be with me. That's why he took the shift at the hospital over Christmas." She cried harder, and I hugged harder.

"Bethany, this is going to sound harsh, but I say it from a place of love. You are impossible to want to be with. You're never happy. You always want more. Matt works his ass off to give you the house, the help, the colonics." I shuddered to think about that treatment.

"I don't actually do colonics. I had one, and it was awful." She scrunched up her nose and shook her head.

"But you keep telling me to get one."

"I wanted a bonding experience." She looked up from under wet eyelashes.

"You wanted to punish me for something."

She fell back to the bed. "Now that I know you're sleeping with your boss, I don't feel so inferior." She gave me a superior smile, but it wasn't her normal I've-got-you-where-I-want-you grin. This one held humor, and I could see she was teasing.

"You gonna tell Dad what you saw?"

She laughed until she claimed she'd pee her pants. "Nope, telling Dad I walked in after his daughter's boss screwed her with his ten-incher isn't something I'm going to do."

"Thank you."

"You know," she said as she stood and pulled me up with her, "it pisses me off that you have a bigger dick than I do."

I gave her a playful punch in the arm. "Oh, Bethany, no one, and I mean *no one*, has a bigger dick than you."

My sister laughed all the way to the bathroom.

I walked back into Mark's room to find it deserted. I picked up my bra and panties and quickly changed out of my snot-soaked sweater and joined the group downstairs.

CHAPTER SIXTEEN

MARK

J ess bounced down the steps like a kid who'd just won the ring toss.

"Everything okay?" her mom asked.

"Yep, it was time for a little housecleaning. We're good." She picked up a cookie from the bottomless plate and flopped down next to me.

"You want a drink?" I pointed to the Macallan 18 on the table.

Jess's mouth dropped open, and she mouthed, *He must like you to pull out the 18.*

I poured her a little in one of the empty tumblers Amy had left. "I'd like to make a toast with Jim's fine scotch."

Amy and Jim came to the coffee table with glasses in their hands. Ben arrived with milk.

"Wait," Bethany said, rushing down the stairs. "I want to toast too." Her eyes were red and swollen, but she bore a genuine smile.

She rushed to the refrigerator and pulled out a soda. We all stood around and stared at each other while I contemplated an appropriate toast. I held up my glass. "Here's to a prosperous New Year. To new experiences. To love. To family." I looked toward Jess. "To possibilities." We raised our glasses and shouted cheers.

"How did that contract you were working on upstairs come together?" Jim asked.

Normally, I wasn't the kind of guy that blushed, but heat suffused my cheeks. "It's—"

"I walked in on them just as they finished up," Bethany interrupted. "I'd say they dotted their i's and crossed their t's. Mark looks like a detail man. I'm sure he gave it his all. Pretty impressive, if you ask me."

A giggle bubbled from Jess until it turned into a laugh. A contagious laugh because Bethany bent over and joined her. Ben had no idea what he was laughing at, but he joined in, and then Jim and Amy followed suit. I was the only one with a straight face, and the picture of my stoic expression caused me to join them. Anyone looking from the outside in would have thought we'd lost our minds or that we were simply a happy family enjoying the holiday. I was glad that it was the latter, not the former.

Once the laughter settled, Bethany took Ben to sit amidst a pile of Legos while the rest of us watched *Miracle on 34th Street* and *Scrooge* and I drew Ben a picture of a racecar for Christmas with an IOU written at the top for a toy of his choice.

When I rose from the couch to turn in for the night, Jim told me to set my alarm for six because he wanted to be on the trail by seven. I'd never hunted for the perfect Christmas tree, but I was pretty sure it could be found at noon just as easily as the break of dawn. However, I was simply a partici- pant in the Stone family's Christmas, and I'd be where they told me.

I walked into my room and breathed deeply. It smelled of Jess and our time together. My dick twitched, remembering how amazing we were together. Not just sexually—though that was the best ever—but even when we just hung out. It was effortless. She made everything easy.

Once I tidied up my bed, I went to shower. I didn't want to wash Jess's essence from my body, but I also didn't want to shower at five in the morning when the house was probably cold and there was a real threat of my nut sack retracting into my body.

My head rested against the cool tile while the hot water sluiced over my back. Everything from the soap to shampoo smelled like Jess.

The shower curtain opened, and there she was naked and smiling. "Can I join you?"

I pulled her inside and held her close to my chest. "For a girl who says no a lot ... you're sure doing a lot of yes actions."

She palmed the soap and washed me. Her hands sudsed up my body while her lips caressed my mouth. "You make me want to be bad. I've done things with you I've never done with anyone else."

"You make me want to be good." I switched places with her so the water washed over her hair. I'd never washed a woman's hair, but I was determined to take care of Jess. She leaned back, and water cascaded down her head, over her shoulders, and across her beautiful breasts. I leaned down and suckled on the hardened rosy tips. I allowed myself just a moment of pleasure and went back to her hair. Any longer, and I'd be deep inside her pounding her against the tile.

My fingers clutched the shampoo bottle like it was a lifeline. Something that grounded me, kept me focused on the task at hand.

"Close your eyes." I moved the shampoo through her hair, keeping the suds from her face.

"I've never had a man shampoo my hair." She leaned back and let the water rinse the bubbles away.

"This is new to me too." I plopped a dollop of conditioner on her hair and smoothed it down to the ends. It smelled like flowers.

"What else haven't you done?" She rinsed off the conditioner and traded me places under the hot stream of water.

"I've never stayed at a parent's house over the holidays. I've never spent the night in bed with a woman. I've never cut down a Christmas tree or suffered through a marathon of holiday movies when all I wanted to do was touch you."

"You could have touched me." She pressed her palms to my chest and let her fingers skate over the prickly hairs.

"And what would your father have said?"

"I guess that depends on what you said. Sometimes silence is the better option." She gave me a quick kiss and stepped out of the shower.

After a final rinse, I followed her. "What do you mean?"

She wrapped a towel around her body and tucked the end between her breasts before handing me my own.

"It's better to say nothing unless we can explain to my parents what this is. And since I'm pretty sure neither of us is certain, it's better to stay quiet. My dad is pretty forward-thinking, but if he thought this was just about sex, I'm not sure he'd understand."

I wrapped my towel around my hips. "This is more, Jess. Definitely more."

"Is it?" She let her towel drop to the floor in front of me. "Would you sleep with me and not have sex? Could you? I mean, we haven't passed a bed yet that we haven't broken in."

She looked down at my tented towel. I was hard. I couldn't help it. She was standing in front of me like Aphrodite, and I wasn't supposed to react? I'd been in that vagina. I'd suckled those breasts. She'd swallowed me. I couldn't be within miles of her and not get hard. That was like putting a bone in front of a hungry dog and expecting him to ignore it. Impossible.

"Game on." The words were out of my mouth before I could explain to my dick that it needed to stand down.

"Really?"

"Whose bed are we sleeping in, sweetheart?"

She towel-dried her hair and walked into her bedroom. Tucked under her pillow was the T-shirt I bought her at the truck stop. She pulled it out and let it fall over her luscious curves.

"Come on, Santa, I'm exhausted." She climbed under the pink bedspread and patted the empty space next to her.

"You know this is cruel and unusual punishment." I raced back to my room and pulled on a pair of shorts Amy had left behind.

"You need reinforcements?" She scooted to the edge of the twin bed, and I climbed in next to her, then pulled her into my embrace. I kept up the internal mantra of "down, boy," but it was no use. Tonight I'd die a slow, hard death.

Jim was like a drill sergeant. He had everyone lined up at the door by a quarter to seven. We were well-fed and well-dressed for subzero weather.

"Good morning, Mark." Bethany breezed by me with a smile. "Would you mind buttoning up Ben? I'm going to grab him a snack in case he gets hungry."

"No problem." I leaned over to Jess and said, "I feel like I'm in the movie *Body Snatchers* and your sister was the first victim."

"Just go with it. It could be fleeting." She dropped to her knees in front of Ben and buttoned him up tight. She pulled him in and kissed him all over his face.

"Gross," he said and squirmed away from her.

I picked the boy up and tapped him on his little pink nose. "Someday you will be praying for a woman as pretty as your aunt to cover your face with kisses."

Just like all little boys did, he shook his head and stuck out his tongue like he was gagging. I laughed because I knew in about ten years I'd be proved right.

We headed out of the house single file with Jess and me pulling up the rear.

"I made it through the night." I pressed my gloved hand to her bottom. It was easy enough to drop if anyone looked over their shoulders toward us.

"Barely. I think I have a bruise where you poked me all night."

"That's just more proof that I desire you but care enough to put my desire aside."

She threaded her arm through mine and laid her head against my shoulder. Once again, being with Jess was easy. She made it feel perfect.

"I'm impressed, Mr. Cantwell. You showed great restraint, but you know what disappointed me the most?"

The fact that she was disappointed in me made my gut clench. I wanted Jess to be happy with everything I did. As much as I'd wanted my dad's approval all my life, I wanted Jess's one hundred times more.

"How did I disappoint you?" I took the risk of stopping and turning her toward me. It was an intimate moment that needed a face-to-face encounter.

She cupped my cheek and smiled. "It was disappointing that you showed great restraint. I was hoping you'd fail." She lifted up on her tiptoes and pecked at my lips.

With a growl to my voice, I whispered in her ear, "Tonight, I'm going to show you what a failure I can be."

We caught up with the others who stood in front of what they called the perfect tree. They walked around it at least a dozen times.

"What do you think, Mark?" Jim asked.

I walked around the tree with an unskilled eye. "The proportions look good. In all honesty, sir, I've never had a Christmas tree so I'm not the one to ask."

A collective gasp sounded from the group.

"Well, son, I think it's time you learned how to celebrate the season." Jim held out the axe for me to take. "Take the first whack at her."

"You think the tree is a girl?" I asked as I palmed the handle of the axe.

"When you see her all dolled up later, there won't be a question in your mind." Jim carved a line in the snow of the trunk and told me to aim there.

It took a dozen swings before Ben yelled *timber* and seven feet of tree fell over. The women clapped their hands and bounced in the snow like they'd just witnessed something wonderful, which I supposed, was part of the tradition. Watching their excitement filled me with warmth; I felt like I was part of something wonderful.

"You girls go on ahead and get the decorations ready. Ben, make sure your mom doesn't eat all the cookies before Mark and I get back," Jim said. He waited until they were out of earshot and then continued, "You're in love with my daughter, aren't you?"

I stood in front of him, frozen like a deer in headlights. How did I answer him? *Honestly* was the only way. "I think I might be."

"Does she know?"

I shook my head. "I haven't told her."

"Don't you think she's worthy of your words?" He picked up the heaviest part of the tree and pointed for me to take the top.

"She's definitely worthy of my words." I hated to turn my back on a man who held an axe, but I also hated to disobey his orders. "I'm not sure I'm worthy of her love."

Jim dropped the tree and came up to stand in front of me. He looked me eye to eye. "No one will ever be worthy of Jess. She's better than you, but you know what? Her mother was better than me. I'm the man I am today because Amy thought I was worth it. Deep inside I knew I wasn't. I'm glad she gave me a chance."

"How did you know she was the one?"

Jim pulled a flask out of his pocket and took a swig before he offered it to me.

"I couldn't think of anything but her. I knew in my heart that nothing was as important as her. I would have given up anything for that woman."

I tipped back the flask, letting both his words and the whiskey burn all the way down to my stomach.

"You think about it long and hard, son." He walked to the front of the tree and picked it up. "You take the heavy end. I'm too old for this shit, but it's important to my girls, so I'll be ninety and still trekking out in the damn cold to cut down the perfect tree."

"Can't you buy one?"

"Sure you can, but it takes something away from the experience. That moment when you come across the one that makes them squeal with happiness is priceless. Traditions are important, Mark. Some you adopt, and some you create. What will your legacy be?" He tucked the flask back inside his pocket. "I'll tell you one thing, my Jess could care less about money. Cut her down a tree, though, and you'll have her heart for life."

I hoisted the trunk of the tree to my shoulder and walked. The journey seemed twice as long on the way back. Maybe because I was halfway to frostbite, or maybe because I was filled with fear that I was in love with Jess and I'd never be enough.

Jim and I brought the tree into the house and set it into the stand, then took a much-needed break while the rest of the family worked like a well-oiled machine. Ben climbed underneath to fill the water reservoir. Amy draped a velvet skirt around the bottom. Bethany circled the branches with twinkling lights. Jess separated the ornaments into thematic piles while I watched in awe.

"Who hangs the first ornament?" Ben asked.

Everyone looked at me. "Oh no, this is your tree," I said and backed away.

Jess pulled me to her and placed a gold colored glass ball in my hand. "This one is always the first. It's gold to signify the value of family."

I held the delicate ball in my hand but felt like it was lodged in my throat. "This is a family tradition. One of you should hang the first ornament."

"Mark," Jim called from his leather throne, "you became family the minute you walked in. Now hang the damn ball because my wife won't feed us until the tree is decorated."

I wasn't an emotional man, and I couldn't remember a time I'd ever cried. But in that moment, my eyes grew wet, and my chest grew tight. After some searching, I decided on the perfect place to hang the ornament of honor: smack dab in the middle of the tree so everyone would see it.

By the way everyone celebrated, you would've thought I'd given birth to Christ. When I turned around, I brushed a tear from my eye. "I think I'm allergic to pine." It was a lame excuse, and surely no one bought it for a second, but no one called me on it either.

While Jim supervised from his chair, we all took turns hanging ornaments until there was more sparkle than tree showing.

"You're right," I said to the man who shared another tumbler of his best scotch with me. "She's quite a beauty."

Jim looked from Bethany to Jess, and then his eyes locked on Amy. "Yes, she is, and the tree ain't bad either."

We all sat down to the pan of lasagna that the women had popped into the oven as we men trekked back, now bubbling and golden on top. Then it was back to Christmas duties: Amy baked more cookies for Santa; Ben placed his heartfelt and handmade gifts under the tree; and I retrieved the few things Jess had for her parents and sister, tucking them and my picture for Ben between the other gifts.

Ben and I went outside and sprinkled carrots on the snow-covered yard because the reindeer would be hungry. A plate of cookies and a glass of milk were put by the fireplace. The fire had long ago been tamped out because Santa would be coming down the chimney and he wouldn't leave presents if he got his bottom burned.

It took forever for Bethany to get the little guy to sleep, but once he was out, the grown-ups enjoyed some adult eggnog. Jim tapped on his computer while Amy was glued to a classic Christmas movie. With everyone occupied, it was time for Jess and me to follow Ben's lead.

I threaded my fingers through Jess's as we walked up the stairs. If anyone cared, we didn't hear a peep, and the important thing was that *we* didn't care.

"Mark," Jim called from his leather Lazy Boy.

We stopped at the top of the steps waiting for him to comment on our exodus. "Yes, sir." I peeked over the rail where he looks up from his computer.

"The main pass just opened."

"Thank you, sir." I turned and led Jess to my room. I tried to shut the door, but it caught on something. Above the frame was a plastic piece of greenery.

"Mistletoe." I plucked it from where it was taped. "Did you do this?" I held it over her head and nipped at her lips.

She wrapped her arms around my neck. "No. I was with you the whole time. It must have been Bethany."

"I was doing a great job of disliking your sister, but I can't anymore. There's good left inside of her. What did you guys talk about that changed her tune?"

"She just realized that there wasn't anything more important than family."

I kissed Jess like it was my last kiss to give. "Stay with me tonight. Let me love you."

"I wouldn't want to be anywhere else."

I removed her clothes one piece at a time and made love to her slowly. I told her with my body what I wasn't ready to say with my words. She deserved all three words, but I couldn't give them to her yet. Tomorrow I'd heal the wounds of my past, and I'd be ready to move on with my future. A future with Jess.

CHAPTER SEVENTEEN

JESS

I woke to the rustling of fabric. Backlit by the bathroom light, Mark straightened his tie and slipped on his jacket. I swallowed the lump lodged in my throat. I knew the minute he walked out the door, nothing would be the same. Gone would be the man who teared up placing his first ornament on the tree. There wouldn't be any more plaid flannel or Doc Martens. By next week, we'd be back at sea level, and these perfect days would be a memory.

"You have everything you need?" My voice caught in my throat, and I hoped it sounded more tired than upset.

"Well, you're not coming with me, so there's that." He sat on the edge of the bed, his face freshly shaved with a borrowed razor, his hair no longer sex-messy but neatly combed and boardroom-worthy. "I'll call you when I get there."

"Okay."

He pressed his lips to mine, and when he pulled away, I curled into the comforter to cover the tears I couldn't control. I had no right to ask him to give up what he'd been trying to get back for over a decade. I could never understand what it meant to him. Even at her worst, Bethany wouldn't stoop so low as to take something from her family.

"I'll see you soon, sweetheart. Merry Christmas."

I counted all fourteen steps that he walked down, hoping on each one that he'd stop and turn around. I listened as the front door opened and closed. As the icy snow crunched under his Italian loafers. As the beat-up rental whined to life and chugged and coughed all the way down the driveway. I tried to convince him to take Dad's Jeep but he said my parent's had given him enough already.

I buried my head in my pillow and cried harder than I'd ever cried in my life. Light leaked into the room from the hallway.

"Are you okay?" Bethany climbed into bed beside me. She wrapped me in her arms and hugged me tight. "He'll be back."

"No, I don't think so." I pulled the edge of my T-shirt up to wipe my eyes. "I'll see him back in Los Angeles, but it won't be the same."

"Why would you say that? It's obvious the man loves you."

I rolled back and stared at the ceiling. "Mark loves his business more than he could ever love me." I hugged the pillow that still smelled like him. "We'll get back to Los Angeles, and he'll go back to his boardroom ways."

Bethany lifted up on one arm. "Here's where I give you some sisterly advice. Men don't think with their hearts. They think with their egos and their dicks, and if Mark's ego is as big as his penis, then he's going to need some time coming to terms with his feelings for you."

"Do we have to keep talking about the size of him?"

Bethany laughed, and then covered her mouth so she wouldn't wake Ben, who was sleeping only a few doors down. "Yes, I'm still pissed at you about that. Seriously, how in the hell did you get so damn lucky?"

"You call this lucky? Look at us. It's Christmas morning, and the men we love are somewhere else. Yours gets a pass because he's probably saving someone's life. Mine … I get it. I get him, but a part of me hoped against hope that he would stay." That realization made me feel awful too because I knew how important this deal was for him.

"Just remember that men are inferior species. Knowing that makes me feel better." Bethany gave me a squeeze and rolled out of bed. "I can't lay in this bed with you anymore. I just know you had hot monkey sex all night, and it feels icky knowing I'm lying where he …"

I picked up Mark's pillow and tossed it at her. "Get out of here." I rolled over and pulled the covers to my nose. They still smelled like him.

"Don't get too comfy. You've got about an hour before an excited four-year-old wakes up the house with a scream."

I closed my eyes and sank back into sleep, but like Bethany warned, the ear-piercing scream came in loud and clear, though it wasn't as timely as she'd predicted. It was well past eight. The morning light shone through the seams of the curtains, casting a beam on Mark's borrowed clothes. He'd folded them neatly and placed them on the dresser. It was as if he'd never been here and they were still waiting for his arrival.

With all the commotion downstairs, I knew I wouldn't be allowed a second longer than it would take for me to get dressed. I pulled on the borrowed jeans. I was halfway to wearing the ugly snowman sweater when I decided I wasn't ready to let Mark go yet. He might not have been present in person, but I'd make sure he was present in my heart. I shook out the black T-shirt and pulled it over my head. Next, I shrugged on the flannel shirt that hung to my knees. With a final look back at the bed we'd made love in last night, I squared my shoulders and walked down the steps.

It was eerily quiet for a house with an excited four-year-old. I turned the corner and heard Ben giggle from behind the kitchen island.

"Why is everyone hiding?" I could see my mom's blonde hair peeking out from behind the sofa. My dad's Santa hat popped up above his lounger. Movement came from behind the tree, and I was sure it was Bethany. "Come out here before you knock over the tree. What the hell are you all doing? This isn't how we do Christmas."

The arm of a finely tailored suit peeked out from the side of the tree. Inch by inch Mark appeared. On top of his head was a set of reindeer ears. "Merry Christmas, sweetheart."

I collapsed in a heap in the middle of the floor and cried. My family bolted from their hiding places to scream "Merry Christmas!" Mark scooped me up and pulled me to the couch where he cradled me in his lap.

"I thought you were in Aspen." I wiped my tears and runny nose on his plaid shirt.

"I got within a few miles and turned back." He looked at my father. "A wise man recently told me I'd know I was in love when nothing else mattered but her. Each mile I drove made my heart ache. It was like I left pieces of my heart behind. By the time I got to the city limits, my chest cavity was empty."

He slid me off his lap and dropped to his knees in front of me. "I don't have anything to give you for Christmas but words. I hope they'll be enough." He pulled my hands to his heart. "I love you, Jess Stone. I've loved you since that day you walked into my office and told me I couldn't live without you. You were right. I was just too stupid to know."

My sister chimed in, "Told you … inferior species."

"Can I dislike your sister sometimes?"

I pulled Mark into the seat next to me. "Of course, but not today because today is all about family. Look around you. This is what life is about. You can't make a diamond without coal. Bethany's a diamond in the rough."

"Which means she's still coal," Jim said. "We keep hoping Matt can put enough pressure on her to make her shine."

Bethany spread her arms wide. "I may be coal, but this guy—" She wrapped her arms around Ben. "—he's the diamond."

Ben wriggled out of her arms and raced to the front of the tree, shaking with anticipation. "Can I hand out presents?"

"Of course, honey," Amy said. "Start with your mom, we promised her the first gift."

Ben let out a disappointed growl and handed his mom his handmade gift, wrapped in newsprint and tied with string.

She started to open it and stopped. "Not today. I think Mark should open his gift first." From under the tree, she pulled a long heavy package.

Dad sat on the edge of his seat and watched with interest. "Come on, Uncle Mark. Open it. Hurry."

Mark ripped through the wrapping to find Dad's ax. He looked up at my father, and a tear fell from his eyes. "I don't understand. How did you know I'd be back?"

Dad rose from his seat and tugged Mark in for a man hug. The one-handed, pat-on-the-back kind that said it all in their caveman language. "Because you love my daughter, and you're worthy of her. Besides, I'm getting too old for that cold shit, and someone else needs to take over that family tradition. Are you up for it, son?"

"Damn pine allergy." Mark swiped at his wet lashes. "I'll make you proud."

Dad gave Mark another pat on the back. "You already have, son. You already have. Now let's open some presents, shall we?"

The next twenty minutes was a flurry of paper and bows. Bethany surprised me again with a gift that made sense. I opened the box to find a beautiful leather satchel.

"Every secret—" She rolled her eyes. "—administrative assistant should have a briefcase of sorts."

I slipped a check for thirty-five hundred dollars into her back pocket before we handed our parents the tickets to an Alaskan cruise. Bethany had been right again. They were thrilled and spent the next hour exclaiming over the brochure.

Mom and I made our way to the kitchen to start breakfast while Mark, Dad, and Ben cleaned up the paper. It was fun watching the two men pretend to bury Ben and then call out for him. I wasn't sure who had more fun, Mark or Ben. Bethany sat at the center island and buttered toast.

"Oh my God, I forgot your present." I dropped the whisk and raced to get my purse from upstairs. When I got back downstairs, I demanded, "Why didn't you remind me?"

She tilted her head and smiled. "I'm trying to turn over a new leaf."

I held the pretty blue box behind my back. "Pick a hand."

"Right."

"No." I switched hands just to irritate her.

"Left."

"Wrong again." I palmed the gift and held it out. "This gift is held in my heart."

I dropped the Tiffany's box into her palm and watched her jaw drop with it. "You shopped at Tiffany's?"

I pulled the top off the box to show her the Christmas tree charm. "I couldn't give you the stationery I'd already bought."

We both laughed until we cried. The front door burst open, and the brisk cool air rushed past us. "Ho ho ho," came a deep voice from the entry. We all turned and watched Matt rush in to scoop up his wife and son.

"I can't live with you, but I'll be damned if I can live without you, either." Matt pulled Bethany in for a kiss while Ben made gagging noises.

I took the precocious four-year-old from his father's arms. "Go to Uncle Mark so your parents can have a moment together."

Mark sat on the floor with Ben in his lap. I leaned across the island and watched as the two played together. This was the boy Mark should have been able to be. The kid who sat in front of a Christmas tree and experienced the joy of the season. Instead, he was forced to skip an entire rite of passage and be a man.

He must have felt my eyes on him because he looked up at me. "Can I make my list for Santa now? I want one of these." He held up the erector set and smiled.

CHAPTER EIGHTEEN

MARK-SIX MONTHS LATER

I pressed the intercom. "Jess, can you come in here?"

She hated when I used the intercom, and I used it just to annoy her because make-up sex on the desk was so amazing.

"Did you really just summon me?" She marched behind my desk and pulled the phone cord from the wall.

"I did." I leaned back in my chair and kicked up my feet on top of the desk. "I needed to see you."

She fisted her hips and narrowed her eyes. "You could have walked out to my desk."

"But I wanted to show you something." I stood up and tugged on the crotch of my pants.

"Really? You're going to summon me to your office and then try to seduce me with your magic penis?"

I rounded the desk and pulled her into my arms. "So it's magic now?"

Her soft curves melted into my hard angles. "It must be. How else do you suppose I got pregnant while on the pill?" She rubbed her still flat tummy. Just barely three months along, she hardly showed any signs that the start of our family was growing inside her.

With my hands wrapped around her back, I held her to me. "In reality, there is a low percentage failure rate, but if you want to believe I have a magic penis, I'll go with that." I pressed against her, forcing her back—step by careful step— until the back of her knees hit my chair. "Have a seat, love."

She leaned back and kicked her legs up on the table, giving me the perfect view, and I groaned. "How am I supposed to concentrate when you're not wearing underwear?"

Her laughter was a song in my heart that I'd never be able to silence. She lived and breathed in me. "How am I supposed to not murder you when you insist on using that damn intercom?"

I licked my lips. "You know I use it because it riles you up, and then I get to calm you down." She watched my tongue with interest.

She dropped her legs to the floor and leaned toward me. Her face was in line with my zipper. She tucked her fingers into my waistband and pulled me forward. "You know it doesn't really bother me." My belt was the first thing to go, then she moved on to my trousers, drawing my zipper down tooth by tooth. "You're so damn perfect that I don't have much to complain about." She slipped her hand into my pants and stroked my raging hard-on. The woman could cough and I'd think it was sexy. She merely breathed in my direction, and I was hard. "Now what did you want?" Up and down her fingers caressed my length. "I've got work to do. My boss likes his lunch on time…served on my naked body."

I thought about yesterday's lunch of dim sum. An uncontrollable twitch rocked me. "Yes, I do, and I'm starving, so I'll get on with it." As much as it pained me to pull her hand out of my pants, I had to. I'd never accomplish anything beyond our orgasms if I let her continue. I reached across the desk for an envelope and placed it in her palm, the same one that had driven me to distraction seconds before.

My mind raced between options. Make love, then open the envelope. Open the envelope, then make love. Screw the envelope and make love. In the end, the envelope was too important. "I've decided to change the logo for the company, and I want your opinion."

She slid her finger under the flap and pulled out the artwork proposal. She stared at the new logo that said *Cantwell and Cantwell* and then dropped the envelope to look at me.

"Who's the other Cantwell?"

I dropped to my knees in front of her. Bethany wasn't the only one to get excited over a blue Tiffany box. Jess's hands shook so badly she couldn't open it. I opened the lid and my heart at the same moment, hoping that she'd accept what I offered her—which was everything I had.

"Jess Stone, you walked into my office and kidnapped my heart. You're having my child, and I hope you'll take a package deal and have me too."

I hadn't acquired my grandfather's company after all—when they said it was Christmas Day or bust, they weren't kidding —but looking into Jess's eyes I knew I'd acquired something far better—her love.

I took the ring and slid it on her finger. It was nowhere near as pretty as her, but her tears told me she liked it (or that she was as allergic to big diamonds as I was to pine needles).

In my mind, yes was the only acceptable answer, and I knew it was exactly the word she'd give me because on Christmas morning last year, I'd become a part of her family, and that made me gold in her eyes. Or at least a piece of coal worthy of a good shine.

She fell into my arms, and I took us both to the floor where I worshipped her body for hours. The phones went unanswered and knocks on my door were ignored because every minute with Jess was the most important minute of my life.

CHAPTER NINETEEN

JESS - SIX MONTHS LATER

W e arrived in Denver on a sunny afternoon. The day was so different from last year. The skies were blue. The roads were clear. The air was crisp, but it couldn't be considered cold.

Mark drove the SUV up the mountain toward my parents' house. He tried to bypass the truck stop, but I wanted a new *I put out for Santa* T-shirt. Mine had long ago given up the fight to cover my burgeoning belly. Our son was due any day, and although my husband and my doctor weren't keen on travel this late in my pregnancy, their arguments fell on deaf ears. Christmas was for family, and I wasn't going to miss a day with mine.

When we passed by the motel where it all began, I begged him to stop and rent our room for old times' sake, but he said he'd feel better once we got to our destination.

When we pulled in front of my parents' house, I waddled to the front door and was immediately wrapped in the loving arms of Mom and Dad until Dad abandoned the too-long hug to help Mark with our bags. We had six of them: four filled with presents and two for clothes.

Matt and Bethany were already there with Ben, who seemed to have grown a foot since we last saw him at our wedding.

"God, I hate you," Bethany said. She rubbed her own growing belly and looked at mine. "You have that pregnancy glow people talk about. I never get that. I get the puke-green sheen from months of throwing up. Green is not my color."

"Don't be silly, you look great in green," I told her.

While Bethany and I kicked back in the loungers, Christmas came into focus with Mom making cookies, the boys cutting firewood, and the television playing a marathon of movies.

The next morning, we were lined up at the door by seven, ready to find the perfect tree. Mark carried the ax my father handed down to him last year with pride.

When the perfect tree was found, Dad marked the spot to cut, and my man swung the ax. He passed the ax to Matt, wanting to share the moment. Swing by swing, the trunk slowly weakened until eight feet of Douglas fir hit the ground.

The family cheered, but the sound that came from my mouth was more of a squeal. I pasted a smile on my face as the first contraction wrapped around my stomach and threatened to gut me.

"Hurry," I said as sweetly as possible.

No one paid attention.

"Hurry," I growled like a woman possessed. Everyone turned. "Please hurry." My smile was forced like a kid posing for class pictures.

"You okay, baby?"

"Hurry, hurry, hurry," I panted.

"Oh shit. It's time," Bethany said. "Dad and Matt, get the tree." She delegated like a drill sergeant. "Mom, go ahead of us and get the car warmed up." She looked at Ben and shook her head. He was still too young to be useful. "Mark, pick up your wife and get her to the house."

Everyone raced to do her bidding. Several steps behind us, I heard Bethany sing-song the words, "I'm going to be an aunt! I'm going to be an aunt."

At 12:45 on Christmas morning, Marcus James Cantwell (named after my two favorite men) let out a scream to inform the world that he'd arrived. Although his hair was dark, his eyes newborn blue, and his skin cotton candy pink, he had the glow of a little golden nugget because he was family and family was gold.

He wrapped his little hand around his daddy's finger while he wrapped himself around my heart.

A SNEAK PEEK INTO COLE FOR CHRISTMAS

I had a feeling my life was going to change from the moment I woke up. It could have been wishful thinking, but the sun was brighter and the air crisper. Maybe it felt different because I was desperate for change.

I pulled in front of 35 Thunder Ridge Lane and allowed myself a moment of unbridled envy. The multistory stone and timber home stood by itself at the end of Thunder Bowl. It was the perfect ski-in and ski-out home. In the distance, snowboarders raced down the mountain at breakneck speed, kicking up clouds of powder in their wake. The bowl was for daredevils and pros not beginners like me.

When the owner had called, he'd been desperate for a decorator, and I'd been desperate for a paycheck. Breaking into the Aspen scene had been impossible. Since my arrival early last summer, I'd been shunned at every turn. Tight-knit communities full of rich people didn't open their homes or wallets to strangers.

I hoped the housekeeper had left the key by the front door as promised. I had three days to transform this house into a winter wonderland, and I'd need every minute. Mr. Cole's family was arriving December twenty-third, and he wanted his house decked for Christmas. His exact words were, "I want to give Norman Rockwell a run for his money."

As promised, the key was tucked into the topiary by the front door. It slid smoothly into the lock and with a gentle turn, the door fell open. *Wow.* The great room was . . . well . . . great. So great time stilled as I took in the grandeur of a home many could appreciate but few could afford.

A stone fireplace stretched from the hardwood floors all the way to the twenty-foot beamed ceilings. The sixteen-foot tree I'd purchased today would be perfect tucked between the fireplace and the wall of glass.

It took pinching myself to be certain I wasn't dreaming. I was really in this house, doing this job, *and* earning a paycheck. Out of habit, I began to mentally note my plan of attack. It would take several hours to put the tree together before I could get to the fun stuff—decorating. If the temp agency came through, that time would be cut in half. Hired help was a luxury I couldn't afford, but efficiency was worth the price, and an extra body would be a boon.

Thankfully, Mr. Cole had given me an ample budget. I didn't blink an eye when the tree cost around three thousand dollars. A good quality tree would last many years.

I hoped this job would be my breakout project. It was also my ticket to making it through the winter. I refused to fail. To crawl back to Los Angeles and beg Ryan for help would be unbearable. I couldn't imagine bringing myself so low. I left with my clothes, my car, and my dignity, and now realize I don't need much more than that.

Note to self, *never* sleep with the boss again.

"Hello," a deep voice called from the front door.

I whipped around to see tall, dark, and muscular. "Thank the Lord. I'm so glad you're here." I tossed him the keys. "Open the trailer and start by bringing in the tree. It's in the five boxes toward the back." He hardly seemed prepared for the task. Dressed in khakis and a button-down shirt, he looked more suited for selling the house than decorating it.

I'd expected a long-haired ski bum, not a down-on-his-luck pretty boy. I hoped the man could work because I had no intention of going easy on him since he failed to dress for the job. However, those muscles would be an asset.

"I'm—" He reached to shake my hand, but I shook my head and pointed toward the door.

"We can get chummy later. Right now I need you to get the tree out of the trailer." Surprise lit his eyes. "I have three days to get this house ready. When Mr. Cole brings his family here, I want them to feel like Christmas couldn't exist anywhere else." He was standing there looking at me like I'd grown antlers. If he didn't step into gear, I'd have to send him packing. I wasn't going to pay for lackluster performance. "Move it." And he was out the door.

I suppose I should have let him introduce himself. I would remedy that as soon as he brought the first box through the door. It's not my norm to be rude, but the hours would evaporate if I dallied, and a rushed job was never a good job.

While he muscled the tree boxes from the trailer, I muscled the furniture into a new Christmas-tree-friendly arrangement.

The fireplace and tree had to take center stage. However, the large A-frame window was too beautiful to ignore.

Whoever decorated this space originally did an outstanding job. The furniture was versatile and worked well when separated. The soft leather sofa was a perfect fit in front of the fireplace. With the massive tree to the right it would be a comfortable place to camp out on Christmas morning and open presents.

I closed my eyes and visualized it complete. Flickering lights. Festive bulbs. Family. All necessary ingredients for a memorable holiday.

"Where do you want the first box?" The man had a sexy-as-all-get-out voice. The kind that made you clench your thighs and need to change your underwear.

"Bring it here. By the way, I'm Chloe Craig, but most people call me Cici. I'm sorry I was so rude earlier. You have no idea how important this job is to me. It's been hard to get a foothold in the industry here, and this job is like getting a golden ticket."

"Elias, my name is Elias." He stopped at his first name and that worked for me. The less chitchat the better.

"Well, Elias, seeing you come through the door made my day. I wasn't sure the service would send someone." Something flashed across his face. I wasn't sure what I'd seen in his eyes, but I would have sworn it was humor. "It looks like Tannenbaum Temps has done me a solid." Maybe like me, he was happy to be employed.

"Where do you want this?" He pushed the box across the floor until I bolted forward and threw myself on top to stop him.

"No, you could scratch the floor. This is a multimillion-dollar home, and let me tell you, you may look like you could live here, but neither of us can afford to refinish these floors." I circled him to look for damage. No scratches. *Whew.* "Rich people don't take kindly to employees ruining their homes. If you're going to work with me, you're going to have to pay closer attention to our client's belongings."

"Duly noted." He groaned while he hefted the box off the floor and carried it to the window.

"Those shoes are going to kill your feet by the end of the day." He stared down at his leather loafers and shrugged. "If you hope to work with me again, I suggest you work hard today and think about dressing more appropriately tomorrow." I wasn't sure he was going to work out, but I'd be darned if I sent him home before the heavy lifting was done. Besides, he was easy on the eyes.

I pulled a scrunchie from my pocket and twisted my hair into a high ponytail. Not the most flattering look, but one that made sense for a full day's work. I didn't have the time or patience to deal with my out-of-control hair. I suppose I should be grateful I'd inherited the Craig curls. I was low maintenance: just wash, toss, and go.

While Elias left to get the next box, I thought through my plan of attack and began.

The base to the tree fit perfectly into the space I'd chosen. I began to insert the color-coded branches into their corresponding colored slots. Elias continued to carry in boxes. I was on number two when he had carried in box five. His poor shirt was drenched in sweat. Beads of perspiration rolled down his face and dripped from his dark curls onto his collar. I was tempted to reach up and wipe his brow. The poor man looked miserable. He was obviously not used to manual labor, and I wondered why Tannenbaum sent him. I was sure I'd put heavy lifting in the job description. I couldn't fault his work though; he was quick and didn't complain.

"On the front seat of my SUV is a cooler with a variety of drinks from water to soda. Help yourself." I turned around and went back to placing branches into their slots. He walked toward the door, and I called to him, "After you get a drink, bring in the ladder. We'll need it to assemble the rest of the tree."

He lugged in the ladder and set it up next to the tree. I loved that I didn't have to tell him what to do. I'd worked with some clueless people, and often it took more time to explain than to do the job myself. Today was looking up. It was a bit rocky at first. Just goes to show you, you shouldn't judge a person by their Italian loafers.

"What does a tree this size cost?" He pulled a branch from the box and looked for its color-coordinated slot.

"These run anywhere from twenty-five hundred up to the tens of thousands. I was able to get this one for just under three grand with it being so late in the season. I used my designer's discount and got an extra ten percent off." I tugged the next section out of the box and climbed the ladder to slide it into the existing pole. The tree was well over seven feet at this point but we still had nine feet to go.

"So will you charge your client the original amount and pocket the rest? That would seem the prudent thing to do." He stood by the ladder and steadied it as if he were afraid I'd fall. Hell, I'd spent half my life on ladders.

"No way. I always pass on the discount to my client. The ten percent is nothing, but a follow-up job is everything. Hand me the red-coded branches."

He began to hand them to me one by one. Thankfully, his sweaty face had dried, and the red had left his neck. The last thing I needed was pretty boy to get overheated and need medical attention.

"What do you do for a living, Elias? You're doing a fine job, but this obviously isn't in your lane." I pulled the branch from his hand and giggled at his look of surprise.

"I'm not sure if I should be pleased or offended."

"Don't be offended. Look at your hands. There isn't a callous anywhere, and you have fingernails prettier than mine. I should be offended." I shoved another branch into the center pole. We were making quick work of the tree.

"I can't lie to you. I'm more an office worker than a manual labor kind of guy, but I'm not afraid of getting my hands dirty."

"I got that impression." I brushed the sweat off my forehead and wiped my hand on my jeans. I always dressed clean but casual for my job. Today was no different. The polo shirt I wore had Craig Designs above the left breast. It felt good to represent myself rather than Ryan Westland Design Company.

For the next hour we worked side by side, assembling branch after branch. I placed the perfectly pointed pine branch on top. The way it filled the space was perfect. Mr. Cole had a good eye for measurements, as it was the exact height needed for the room. He'd said the ceilings were about twenty feet high, and he was spot on.

"What do you think?" I stood back and admired our work. It looked great now, but once it was decorated, it would be breathtaking.

"It's all right." He shrugged his shoulders and walked to the wall of windows. He was obviously not a man who appreciated the holidays.

"This is going to come out great. I'm glad the owner isn't present. I hate it when they're around. It slows down the process. Normally, I wouldn't take on a house sight unseen, but the poor man sounded desperate, and I was equally desperate for a job."

He'd said he was out of town and his girlfriend had dropped the ball. The phone connection had been bad, but we'd managed to get the details covered before we were disconnected. Since that first call we'd communicated through texting.

"Why so desperate?" He turned to look my way. Too bad the guy was broke. He would have made good dating material. Shame I couldn't afford to take care of both of us.

"I had a falling out with my last company and moved to Aspen for a fresh start. This is my first job."

"Welcome to Aspen. Do you ski?" His question caught me by surprise. I suppose it shouldn't have since he was looking longingly out the window at the ski run. People like us couldn't afford to ski. We watched while others raced down the slopes.

"I don't think what I do can be called skiing. I imagine I'm more of a snowplower than an actual skier. You?" I began to fold down the boxes to get them out of the way. It was time for the fun to begin.

"Love it. The lessons I took a few years back really helped my form. You should think about hiring an instructor."

I had no idea what he thought I made, but an instructor was out of the question this year. Every dime I earned needed to get me through the winter. I had rent to pay and food to buy, not to mention car payments to be made.

"I'll have to look into that. Can you start bringing in the other boxes? They're full of lights and decorations. I figure if we can get the tree done today, we can work on wreaths and garlands tomorrow. I want to use live materials so the pine smell infuses the air. There's nothing like the smell of pine in winter. I'm also going to use lots of cinnamon sticks so the house smells like freshly baked goods."

"You've got this whole thing down, don't you?" He piled the flattened boxes into his arms and carried them out the front door. Moments later he returned with two full boxes and a bottle of cold water in his back pocket. "Here, you need to stay hydrated. The altitude can really take a lot out of you. Drink up."

I was touched by his consideration, and gladly took the water, gulping down half of it. I was so intent on getting the tree up, I hadn't considered thirst or dehydration.

We took a short break to eat lunch. I happily shared the couple of peanut butter and jelly sandwiches I'd brought with me. He'd come unprepared.

The rest of the job was like opening boxes on Christmas morning. I loved the holidays, and decorating the Christmas tree was always my favorite activity. I usually had a six-footer. Imagine the fun I was going to have with sixteen feet.

Elias looked less than enthused. "Don't you enjoy decorating a tree?" I plugged in the lights and watched them twinkle to life. This tree's stationary and blinking lights would keep it in perpetual illumination.

"I just don't see the point. You spend a ton of time putting something up that you'll just tear down and destroy in a week or so. It seems like a waste of time and resources, but it's important to some people. I get that, so I go with the flow."

"Well, get with the flow and start placing the decorative picks in between the branches. We have garland and ribbon to hang before we get to the bulbs. I think we have a thousand of them to place before we get to the candy canes. Mr. Cole didn't tell me whether there were children or not, but young or old, a tree isn't a tree without peppermint treats."

"I like peppermint." He moved to the opposite side of the tree and began to place the picks.

We spent the next couple hours working from the top of the tree to the bottom. Elias was slow to catch on, but once he did, he seemed to get into the spirit. I played Christmas music from my iPhone, and we hung the tree jewelry to songs like "Deck the Halls" and "Grandma Got Run Over by a Reindeer."

I explained the symbolism of the Christmas tree, and he sounded surprised when I told him the evergreen symbolized undying life. Christmas was about hope and love. Add in everything else like stars and balls, bows and candy canes, and you had an extravaganza of delight.

"Do we have a star?" Did I hear a hint of excitement in his voice?

"Of course we have a star." I pulled out an ornate topper made from pearlized glass. Lit from the inside, it would throw off prisms of light that would shine across the wooden ceiling. The star was a foot tall and would take the height of our masterpiece to seventeen feet.

I offered the star to Elias. He gave me a strange look and shook his head. I pushed the star into his hand and told him to get his ass up the ladder and place the crowning glory on the tree. From his horrified expression, you would have thought I'd handed him a scalpel and told him to perform a triple bypass.

He climbed the ladder slowly. "I don't like heights." His knees wobbled, and his face paled.

I climbed behind him and held on to his shaking calves. Man, he had muscular legs. "You'll go on a ski lift, but you won't climb a ladder?" I wanted to run my hands all the way up his thighs and squeeze the cheeks I knew would be firm under my grasp, but I didn't dare. He was a day hire, and I was his boss.

"I don't look down, and there's a payoff when skiing. Nothing good comes with ladders." He reached up and slid the star over the center. "Why are you so comfortable with heights?" He fumbled with the cord, and I felt his whole body shake while he reached farther to push the plug into the waiting socket attached to the tree.

"My dad's a painter, and I spent my childhood helping him. I grew up on a ladder." Just then, the star lit up, and light shot out from each point, spilling across the room. Breathtaking. Given the bright smile on his face, even Elias seemed to be feeling happy.

We'd put in a good day's work, and I invited Elias to come back tomorrow. He was a hard worker and was open to suggestion. That went a long way with me, but when I asked him to come back he busted into thunderous laughter and told me he would be here. No wonder he was unemployed, he was weird.

He folded the ladder and walked it to my trailer. When he returned, I was sitting on the sofa in a room lit only by the Christmas tree. Stunning. I'd never seen one as beautiful. I knew I could do a good job, but I had no idea how amazing seventeen feet of glass balls, satin ribbon, and peppermint candy could look. I only hoped Christmas joy might reach Elias too. Shame I couldn't help with that.

A SNEAK PEEK INTO THE TROUBLE WITH TINSEL

Tommy lounged sleepy-eyed in front of the television as I whisper-yelled at my mother. "You lied to me." Frustration blazed through me like dry kindling set afire. "You said you fell and broke your arm, and here you sit, decorating cookies?"

Unrepentant, Mom gripped the icing bag in her left hand while her bandaged right wrist sat on the table. "I didn't lie. I slipped on the ice. I thought I'd broken my hand." She dropped the bag, tugged at the binding, and tightened the clip. "It was a serious sprain, Mandy."

I'd do anything for my mother, but I was tired of being manipulated—of people stealing my choices—and my mother was the queen of doing that. All my life, she'd cajoled and nudged, pushing me in the direction that benefited her most. Just when I thought she'd changed…

"I dragged Tommy across the country for a sprain?" I stomped to the old percolator. It burped and spit on the counter while I poured a fresh cup. I needed caffeine, and

Mom needed to move into the present. The past wasn't a place I wanted to dwell upon or repeat.

Cloves, and cinnamon, and hope filled the air. Mom sat at the table and dressed the gingerbread men in white icing pants and button down vests, with delicate, precise movements. When I was a little girl, those scents would dare me to dream that my mother would be like everyone else's mom—that I would walk in the door and she'd want nothing more than to hug me and ask me how I was. But that wasn't the game my mother played. Every smile, every cookie, was a bargaining chip—a way to get me to bend to her will. Yet, here I was, hoping all over again, like a kid who couldn't give up on Santa.

In all honesty, she couldn't help herself. She'd clung to whatever control she could since Daddy died.

"Mom." The hours of travel had roughened my voice. "You called me in tears telling me to come home, the shop would perish without me." I waved my hands through the air as I spoke. I didn't usually act with such flair, but Mom had made it sound like her world would implode without me.

"I can't run the shop with this on my hand." She pulled at the elastic bandage again and sighed. "Besides, it was time for you to come home. You hate New York."

A fact she'd been trying to convince me of since I moved there. "I don't hate New York, Mom." I didn't hate the city; I was indifferent to it. It served its purpose—it was far away from Bell Mountain and it held my job.

In retrospect, being here for two weeks would be a nice respite, but I'd never allow my mother to own that victory.

Mom traded the white icing bag for the red and squeezed out perfect little buttons on the tiny vests. "Bell Mountain is the perfect place to raise my grandson," she whispered, ignoring what I said. She lifted her gaze in Tommy's direction and gave him a nod.

The legs of the chair squeaked as I pulled it from the table and flopped onto the cracked, red vinyl cushion. Mom was stuck in the decade she was born with her diner décor, and black and white checkered flooring. Stuck was something I was familiar with. I hadn't been living my dream. I'd been living in New York and working as a pastry chef for Henry Lefebvre, or as I like to call him, Ornery, and that was no dream. My dreams had died the day a certain man walked out of my life.

Sipping my coffee, I glanced around the kitchen. Nailed to the walls were records by Buddy Holly, Chubby Checkers, and the king himself, Elvis Presley. The chipped jar I painted in fourth grade sat in the corner next to the stove over-flowing with utensils. My elementary school pictures were still taped to the side of the refrigerator. No matter how far I strayed, how crazy she drove me, or how long I stayed away, this would always be home. "You're right, Tommy will love it here, but this isn't permanent. It's just to get you through the holidays." I grabbed the white icing bag from the plate and helped her with the cookies. It was time to let go of my annoyance, and embrace the holiday spirit. Tonight, we were going to decorate the Christmas tree together for the first time since Tommy was born.

"You used to love Bell Mountain too, sweetheart. Everything you could ever want is here." Mom cupped my cheek with her bandaged hand. Her eyes lit up with love.

Not everything, Mom. Bell Mountain had broken me ten years ago when Beau Tinsel left town with his guitar and my heart.

Whoever said picking out a Christmas tree was fun, never did it in subzero weather. Cloudy puffs of steam escaped my mouth each time I breathed. "What about this one?" My teeth chattered while I yanked down Tommy's hat to cover his reddened ears.

Mom, Tommy, and I stood in front of the tree and analyzed it from all angles. "Can't we have a flucked one, Mommy?" Tommy pointed at the tent where a man was glazing a perfect green tree in spongy white material. The fake snow glittered like diamonds under the fluorescent lights.

"It's called flocked, and no, we can't. All white trees belong outside." Surrounded by naturally snow-coated trees, it was overkill to bring a poser into the house. "If you want, we can decorate the pine tree in Grandma's front yard, too. Then you can have a white and a green tree."

My little man jumped up and down with the energy only a child can possess and maintain. "This one's super-duper then."

An uncontainable shiver raced from the tip of my head all the way to my boots. I looked toward my mother, praying she would give her seal of approval before any part of me froze and dropped off. "Okay with you, Mom?"

Mom rounded the tree again. Tommy and I watched as she analyzed each full branch and prickly needle. Just when I thought she'd put a kibosh on it, she smiled and said, "super-duper with me, too. I'll pay." She turned and walked toward the man at the front of the lot.

"Mandy Sawyer?"

I recognized his voice right away. It was pure warmth. "Greg Anderson, how the heck are you?" I wrapped my arms around the boy who'd been my Godsend the last year of high school. We'd stayed in touch for a time, but eventually, I found it easier to sever as many ties with my past as I could. "You're still here?"

Stepping back, I looked at him. He was tall, handsome, and totally not into girls. In fact, Greg Anderson came out on prom night. He was my date, and we had arrived to the dance wearing matching pink gowns. It was a testament to our friendship and a show of solidarity. The fact he had looked better in the dress than I did should have pissed me off, but I could never get angry with Greg. He had been the best boy friend a girl could ever have. And, he was the perfect prom date. He paid for his own dinner, and didn't expect to get lucky in the back seat of his car when the night ended.

He opened his arms with a flourish and looked around him. "I couldn't leave all this behind." He kneeled down in front of Tommy. "And who's this handsome young man?"

Pride radiated from my pores. "This is my son, Tommy." Tommy stared up at Greg and smiled like he was looking into the face of an angel. Greg had that effect on everyone. Something wonderful and happy arrived each time he did. He was hot chocolate on a frigid day and fuzzy socks on a cold morning. He was one of those feel good people.

"Tommy, this is my friend, Greg."

Tommy offered his hand, "I'm Tommy Sawyer, it's nice to meet you." For a six-year-old, he was already a charmer. I'd have to keep an eye on him. With his devilish good looks and charisma, he was bound to break the hearts of many.

Greg raised a single brow in question. "Tom Sawyer? You didn't really do that to him, did you?"

"Do what to me, Mommy?" Tommy looked at me with saucer-sized eyes.

"I named you after a famous character from a book." I gave Greg a little push and a shut-the-hell-up look.

He rose to a towering height and whispered in my ear. "You better teach him to fight."

My mouth dropped open. "Never. He'll be fine. It's character-building."

"Whatever you say." Amusement glinted in his eyes. "Where's his dad?" Greg scanned the tree lot as if looking for someone in particular.

"My dad is famous and very busy," Tommy piped in.

"Is that right?" Greg raised his hand for a high-five. "Right on." He turned to me with an inquisitive tilt to his head.

"No, it's not who you think. It's a long story that's better left for coffee, a pastry, and a warmer environment. What about tomorrow at the Sweet Shop? I'm filling in for Mom over the holidays." It felt funny to think I'd be running the Sweet Shop but oddly comforting as well. Maybe Mom was right; maybe coming home for a while would be good for me.

"I'll be there around four, and I want every sordid detail."

We hugged once more and parted. Despite my misgivings about coming home, the comfort of old friends was encouraging.

After we hefted the tree to the roof of my Jeep, we were on our way. Thankfully, I kept the old heap of junk. It was covered and waiting in the garage for me when I got back into town. After sitting for nearly a decade, it turned over on the first try, proving that not everything from the past would fail me.

———

Once home, I muscled the tree through the front door. A gimpy mother and a little boy weren't much help, but they tried, and I appreciated their efforts. The tree fit perfectly in front of the window, and while I fluffed out the branches, Mom and Tommy sifted through what he called "big CD's." Moments later, the sound of Bing Crosby was crackling and popping on the record player. No digital for Mom. She was old school.

They went into the kitchen to make cocoa while I pulled the old boxes of Christmas decorations up from the basement. Decorating the tree would be a walk down memory lane. Mom never got rid of anything. Whereas she was married to the past, I'd hurled myself into the future, leaving everything behind.

"Are you two ready?" I called from the living room once the lights had been hung from the tree.

"On our way," Mom sang from the kitchen. There was a bit of banging and a lot of giggling coming from their direction, then two elves appeared wearing green and red striped hats and pointed foam ears. The littlest elf carried a plate of gingerbread cookies while the older, supposedly more mature elf brought hot cocoa. A smile lifted my lips. It had been a long time since I'd seen my mom participate in anything joyful. "You two are the cutest in the world." I wiggled Tommy's little nose and told him he got to choose the first ornament for the tree.

He went straight for the homemade decorations. A bejeweled pine cone swung from his little fingers. He held it up and asked who made it. If every ornament needed an explanation, it would be a long night.

"That one was made by your mom with her best friend, Beau. They sat right here in this living room and glued glitter to pine cones. On small pieces of paper, they wrote their secret wishes and tucked them between the scales where they stayed until Christmas morning." Mom was like Dickens; she held the power to mesmerize an audience with the way she weaved a story. Tommy was not immune and his eyes grew wide with curiosity.

"What was your secret wish?" he asked as he hung the glittered pine cone from a center bow. It shimmered under the twinkling lights.

"I can't remember," I fibbed. I remembered exactly what I wished for. I was ten and Beau was eleven. In my best cursive, I wrote that I wanted to grow up and marry Beau Tinsel.

"Of course you remember. How could you forget? That's the one that said you wanted to—"

"Mom!" I stopped her mid-sentence. I didn't want to rehash that memory, and I didn't want to explain Beau to Tommy. What was the point in introducing him to my past—a past that had no influence on Tommy or our future? No, Beau Tinsel was a faint memory, at best.

"What? I was going to say that you and Beau had made the sweetest wishes."

"Did your wish come true?" Tommy pulled a gingerbread man from the plate and licked the red buttons from the vest.

"No, Tommy, my wish didn't come true." My shoulders slumped forward with the knowledge that someday, I'd have to tell him that wishes rarely came true, and life could be hard. At his age, everything was still possible.

Mom picked up the next ornament and hung it toward the top. "The beauty about wishes is, they sit out there and wait for the perfect time to come true, Tommy." She gave me a let-him-dream look and I nodded my head in agreement. There was time enough for the cruelties of the world to rain disappointment on him. For now, let him live in his happy child's world.

"Can we do that, Grandma? Can we decorate pine cones and hide wishes?" Tommy pulled a package of tinsel from the box and stared at his Grandma with expectant eyes. "I have a bunch of wishes."

"As soon as we finish this tree, you and I are going pine cone hunting, we'll let them dry overnight and decorate them tomorrow." Mom's grandma skills stood in direct contrast with her mom skills. With Tommy, she was patient, and playful. With me, adding an "S" before "mothering" nailed it on the head.

Tommy threw tinsel into the air in celebration. It's sparkly strands showered down on everyone. Even a bit hit the tree.

Tommy was having fun and hearing his laughter warmed my heart.

I walked around the tree to the window and wiped the condensation from the pane with my sleeve. The old Victorian across the street stood regal. Its decorative trim and garland-wrapped windows screamed "happy holidays." The icicle lights sparkled like the tinsel on our tree. Through the fogged glass, I reflected on a different time—different Tinsel.

Beau Tinsel had been the love of my life. *Remember me*, he'd said that last night. The next day, he drove away with his guitar in the back seat of his SUV. He headed west and never looked back. That was years ago and my heart still ached.

Mom and Tommy were laughing at the silver strands that decorated the room. The trouble with tinsel was, it was hard to control. It stuck to you or was repelled by you. There was no in-between. It attached to you until something more interesting or electrifying came by. Tinsel was fickle. Tinsel was unpredictable. Tinsel broke my heart.

Mom gathered up the cups from the coffee table when she let it slip. "He's coming back home, you know?"

"Who?" I played stupid. It had been ten years since he'd left, and I hadn't seen him since. The truth was, I'd stalked him on social media, bought every one of his new releases, and even went to a concert when he was performing in New York City.

"Your Beau is coming home. It's time for him, too."

"He's not my Beau, Mom." With my arms crossed over my chest, I asked, "What are you up to?"

"Me?" Her voice swooped low and ended high. She was feigning innocence, but I knew Mom was up to something and if that were the case, Sarah Tinsel was an accomplice. "Did Sarah break her wrist, too?" Beau hadn't come home once since he'd left town. The only thing that would bring him back would be an emergency. I looked heavenward, silently begging her to come clean.

"Oh, heavens no. She twisted her ankle." Mom exited the room laughing.

Hot on her heels, I marched into the kitchen. "Your meddling isn't going to get you anywhere."

"Oh, Mandy, must you act so dramatic. Maybe you missed your calling." She dumped the cups in the sink and proceeded to fill it with hot water and bubbles.

"Mom, you and I both know Beau isn't coming home. He never comes back to Bell Mountain."

"Neither did you, but I got you home." She waved her wounded hand in the air. As usual, not really listening to me. She had already moved on to the next thing. "Tommy, let's go pine cone hunting, and then, you're off to bed, young man. Your mother volunteered to clean the kitchen while we search."

They wrapped themselves in winter gear and disappeared out the back door, leaving me alone with unwelcome thoughts of Beau. If all it took was a twisted ankle to get him back, I should have faked an injury long ago. Sadly, too much time had passed, and our lives had irrevocably changed. He was a star, and I was a single mother. And whatever we might have had between us died a long time ago. I had moved on, moved away from Beau. Still, there were days when the loss weighed heavy on me.

I twisted a piece of tinsel around my finger until the tip turned purple and throbbed. I remembered that feeling well, although last time, I felt it in my heart. Losing Beau was like slowly being suffocated.

For a moment, I stood by the window and watched the house across the street. *Where have you been, Beau Tinsel? Are you really coming home?*

I turned away from the window and curled up in the over-stuffed chair next to the over-decorated tree and sipped my orange, spiced tea. Too many days had been spent in this chair waiting for Beau to return. Too many days wishing for something that would never happen.

Today, I sat and hoped he'd stay away.

GET A FREE BOOK.

BOOK NOOK PRESS

Go to www.authorkellycollins.com

ABOUT THE AUTHOR

International bestselling author of more than thirty novels, Kelly Collins writes with the intention of keeping love alive. Always a romantic, she blends real-life events with her vivid imagination to create characters and stories that lovers of contemporary romance, new adult, and romantic suspense will return to again and again.

For More Information
www.authorkellycollins.com
kelly@authorkellycollins.com

9 781955 379809